"What happened?"

"Pete was here."

"Are you okay?" Matthias asked.

Lily nodded. But she wasn't okay. She was worried about why Pete Peterson kept coming after her and why he wanted the flash drive.

Matthias eyed her cheek. "He hit you."

"He wants the flash drive," she said.

"Any idea why it's so important?"

"Maybe we should look at the files again."

"Do you want to give the flash drive to the deputy?"

Lily thought for a moment and remembered Sheriff Granger's inability to find Noelle Keeper's killer. She didn't value his ability or his determination. "Let's keep the flash drive to ourselves until we can figure out why Pete wants it back."

Matthias raised his brow. "Are you sure that's wise?"

Debby Giusti is an award-winning Christian author who met and married her military husband at Fort Knox, Kentucky. Together they traveled the world, raised three wonderful children and have now settled in Atlanta, Georgia, where Debby spins tales of mystery and suspense that touch the heart and soul. Visit Debby online at debbygiusti.com, blog with her at seekerville.blogspot.com and craftieladiesofromance.blogspot.com, and email her at Debby@DebbyGiusti.com.

Books by Debby Giusti

Love Inspired Suspense

Her Forgotten Amish Past
Dangerous Amish Inheritance
Amish Christmas Search
Hidden Amish Secrets
Smugglers in Amish Country
In a Sniper's Crosshairs

Amish Witness Protection

Amish Safe House

Amish Protectors

Amish Refuge
Undercover Amish
Amish Rescue
Amish Christmas Secrets

Visit the Author Profile page at LoveInspired.com for more titles.

IN A SNIPER'S CROSSHAIRS

DEBBY GIUSTI

LOVE INSPIRED SUSPENSE
INSPIRATIONAL ROMANCE

LOVE INSPIRED® SUSPENSE
INSPIRATIONAL ROMANCE

Recycling programs
for this product may
not exist in your area.

ISBN-13: 978-1-335-58805-0

In a Sniper's Crosshairs

Copyright © 2022 by Deborah W. Giusti

For questions and comments about the quality of this book, please contact us
at CustomerService@Harlequin.com.

Love Inspired
22 Adelaide St. West, 41st Floor
Toronto, Ontario M5H 4E3, Canada
www.LoveInspired.com

Printed in U.S.A.

Giving thanks unto the Father, which hath made us meet
to be partakers of the inheritance of the saints in light:
Who hath delivered us from the power of darkness, and
hath translated us into the kingdom of his dear Son:
In whom we have redemption through his blood,
even the forgiveness of sins.
—*Colossians* 1:12-14

This book is dedicated to my
CRHP Book Club.

Thanks, ladies, for the great reads we've shared,
for the friendship and laughter, and for your support
and encouragement over these past nineteen years.

ONE

Fatigue weighed heavily on Lily Hudson's shoulders as she left Pinewood and drove her taxi along the narrow mountain road to pick up her last customer for the night. A light drizzle of rain pitter-pattered against her car's windshield. Storms were expected to roll through the North Georgia mountains, and after an exhausting weekend shuttling passengers to earn money to pay for her mother's medical needs, Lily longed for a hot bath and a good night's sleep.

Tomorrow was an important day, and she needed to be well rested and ready to confront the painful memories in her past and the people who were determined to ruin her life and her mother's reputation. But first, she had one more fare to transport, a guy whose car had broken down just north of Pinewood.

A crash of thunder and a zigzag of lightning cut across the night's sky, and the rain intensified. Even with her windshield wipers on high, Lily struggled to see and was forced to slow down as she rounded a sharp curve in the winding mountain road.

A white midsize sedan that must have swerved off the road lay at an angle in the ditch. Her heart skittered in her chest as she realized her fare's broken-down car was a more serious situation than a stalled engine or a flat tire. She slammed on her brakes, pulled her taxi to the edge of the pavement, turned on her flashers and stepped out into the wet night. She'd never expected to be the first responder to an accident scene, but surprises came with having her own taxi company, and her first priority was to ensure the man who needed a ride back to Pinewood hadn't been seriously injured.

The big burly and somewhat surly looking guy who stepped around the far side of the sedan appeared unharmed. He was pushing fifty, wore an olive green camo jacket, dark tactical slacks and a military knit cap pulled low on his forehead, and he held a phone to his ear. Relief flashed across his bearded face as he shoved his cell into his breast pocket and motioned her forward.

"I didn't expect you this soon." He grabbed a backpack and duffel bag from the open trunk of the wrecked car.

"Are you okay?" she asked.

"A little shook up but not injured. The road's slick, and I took the turn too fast."

From the skid marks illuminated by her headlights, he had been traveling entirely too fast on the twisting mountain road.

"Have you contacted the garage in town?" she asked.

"My friend Bob is sending a tow truck, but I need to get to a meeting farther up the mountain. He said he called a taxi, which must be you."

Lily hadn't planned on a mountain trip this late at night. "I thought you needed a ride back to Pinewood."

He glanced at his watch. "Actually, I'm headed north to Mountain Crest. Bob should have told you."

"The guy who contacted me said your car had broken down and you needed a ride to the closest town *south* of here. That would be Pinewood."

"Bob's got a problem with directions." The guy narrowed his gaze. "I'm headed north."

She didn't want to argue with a customer, especially one who seemed to have a chip on his muscular shoulders, but navigating the treacherous mountain road this late on a stormy night wasn't what she had in mind when she'd accepted the fare. With a sigh, she thought of Betsy Wyler's letter that she'd shoved into the back pocket of her jeans. Maybe God was ensuring she didn't renege on her own trip to Sunview tomorrow. She had planned to get a restful eight hours of sleep in her tiny but comfortable rental cabin an hour south of Pinewood so she would be fresh to tackle any problems tomorrow might bring.

"I can take you to Sunview. It's about sixty miles from here and the closest town to the north. You can get a room there and catch a ride to Mountain Crest in the morning."

He scowled. Evidently, her customer didn't want to change his plans. Under other circumstances, Lily would have climbed into her car and headed home, but at this time of night, Bob wouldn't be able to find another cab driver interested in taking the man in camo up the mountain. Especially with a storm brewing. As much as she wanted to get home, Lily couldn't leave a stranded motorist to fend for himself on a stormy night.

"Look, Mister…"

"It's…" He hesitated. "It's Peterson. Pete Peterson."

"I doubt your friend will be able to track down any type of taxi or rideshare tonight, but as I mentioned, I'll take you to Sunview."

He shrugged and limped to her car.

"Is your leg hurt?"

"What?" He glanced down. "Ah, no, it's an old wound from the military."

"Army?"

He nodded, threw his gear onto the floor of her car and settled into the back seat. He opened his smartphone and punched in a number. By the time she slipped behind the wheel, he was in a heated conversation with Bob, whoever Bob was.

"Get that tow truck here and haul the car back to the garage. Yeah, I took care of the tags."

Tags? Lily put her car in gear and glanced at the white sedan. Why would the guy remove the car's plate? The only reason that came to mind was he didn't want the sedan traced back to him.

A tingle of concern curled around her neck. She needed to get Mr. Peterson, if that was his name, to the motel on the outskirts of Sunview where she'd say goodbye and good riddance. Then, she'd call the B and B in town and inquire whether they had a room she could rent for the night. What would it hurt to spend tonight in town? Although, if she thought back to all that happened five years ago, she could easily talk herself out of going anywhere near Sunview. The embarrassment and rejection she and her mother had endured, as well as the way she had treated her once-upon-a-time friend on that fateful night still weighed heavy on her heart.

Lily pulled in a deep breath and tightened her grip on the steering wheel. After reading Betsy's recent letter, she'd realized that the past needed to be settled once and for all, no matter how much she wanted to pass that responsibility on to someone else. As the only child of a single mother, the task of clearing her mother's name fell squarely onto her shoulders.

The clock on her dash read ten o'clock as she started her meter. Sunview was more than an hour's drive up the mountain, and Mountain Crest was two-hours farther north. What kind of a meeting took place that late at night, especially in rural Georgia where everything folded up, including the sidewalks, by nine o'clock?

Peterson disconnected from Bob with a perturbed grunt and unzipped his duffel. Flicking her gaze to the rearview mirror, she spied the stock of a rifle poking out of his bag. Evidently, Pete was a hunter, which wasn't unusual in this part of the country.

He rooted around in his duffel, zipped it up again and rummaged in his backpack. After retrieving an older model phone, he plugged in a number. Strange that the guy had a smartphone and a cheaper disposable mobile device.

A voice answered. She couldn't tell if it was

male or female, but whoever it was sounded angry. Glancing again at the rearview mirror, she watched Pete grimace.

"Yeah. I'm on schedule. Is everything set on your end?"

He looked up, caught her gaze in the mirror and pursed his lips. "I'll call you back."

Tucking his phone into his jacket, he sniffed. "Any chance you work with a dispatcher who might know someone else available to drive me to Mountain Crest tonight?"

She didn't want to tell Pete she worked alone. "Sunview has a taxi service, although I'm not sure they take fares this late at night. There's a motel on this road, and the Christmas Lodge is located some distance north of town. Both places should have the phone number for the local taxi service. The motel would be the best deal for the price. It's not as upscale as the Christmas Lodge, but it's clean, and from what I've heard, the manager provides a great breakfast."

Pete bristled. "Why did you mention the Christmas Lodge?"

"I thought maybe you're planning to attend the Christmas festival." Hoping to calm his agitation, she continued, "People come from all over. The evening performance is spectacular. There are fireworks and usually a special entertainer. This year, a singer who grew up in Sunview and made it big in Nashville is coming back to perform. Clay Lambert."

"I've never heard of him."

"Really? He's a nice guy. I knew him in high school. Raised by a single mom, he didn't have anything when he started, but his tunes top the charts now. In fact, the local radio station is featuring his albums in anticipation of the festival."

She clicked on the radio. Static growled, then the heart-wrenching chords of a country Western song filled the car.

"'Home in Time for Christmas' is Clay's latest release," she told Pete. The song was one of Lily's favorites, not that she wanted to return to Sunview for Christmas. If she couldn't get a room at the B and B tonight, she'd drive two hours south to her cabin without even a backward glance. She almost groaned aloud when she realized Betsy was right. She needed to clear the air about what had happened five years ago, even though she wished the painful memories of growing up in Sunview could remain buried.

Pete settled into the seat and seemed to relax as the station continued playing Clay's songs. The storm abated, and the miles passed in relative quiet except for the sound of the country Western star's plaintive voice.

About five miles from town, static rumbled from the radio, followed by the breathy voice of the announcer. "We interrupt this program for a news alert. A stolen white sedan, license plate—" the announcer rattled off the number "—was last seen heading north on Georgia 400. The driver is armed and dangerous."

Lily's pulse kicked up a notch. White sedan? Just like the car Pete had driven. Surely, there had to be hundreds of similar cars on the road. Still, the missing tags came to mind.

"We're almost to Sunview." She turned off the radio and pointed to the surrounding hills bathed in darkness. "The Amish live around here, but you'll have to wait until morning to see their farms."

"Look, lady, why don't you turn onto that dirt road just ahead and let me out there."

"What?"

"You've already done more than enough," he insisted.

No matter his rational, she didn't want to stop on a desolate dirt road. "It's not a problem. We'll be at the motel in a few minutes."

A click sounded from behind her, and a raised pistol appeared in her peripheral vision.

"Make the turn," he growled.

Her mouth went dry, and her pulse raced as a number of scenarios flashed through her mind.

None of them good. Without a doubt, the guy planned to steal her car. Killing her might also be an option.

"Turn now," he warned as they neared the narrow dirt road flanked on both sides by a dense forest.

Lily swallowed hard, accelerated into the turn and swerved into a thick stand of trees. The front left bumper skidded into the trunk of a massive oak tree. Lily's head slammed back against the seat. In the rear, Pete moaned.

Grateful that the airbags hadn't activated, she grabbed the keys from the ignition, threw open her door and started running.

Pete lurched from the car and fired. A round whizzed past her head. She angled deeper into the woods. Another round hit a nearby tree. Bark shattered, striking her like shrapnel. Her cheek stung from the barrage of wood chips. She rubbed her face and gasped when the keys slipped through her fingers.

Stooping down, she raked her hand through the thick floor of pine straw and dried leaves. Her pulse raced, and a roar filled her ears. *Where are the keys?*

Pete's footsteps drew closer.

She sprinted forward.

"Stop, lady. I won't hurt you."

Liar, liar, pants on fire. She wanted to scream

the childhood verse as she raced faster. The terrain was uneven. Her foot caught on a fallen branch, and she landed on her knees.

"Umph." Scrambling to her feet, she continued.

He was behind her, closing in. She could hear his raspy inhale and exhale of breath as well as the erratic cadence of his lopsided gait.

Another round fired. This one grazed the top of her shoulder.

She groaned with pain. Blood dampened her blouse. Suddenly woozy, she staggered forward, lost balance and tumbled down a steep embankment. Her head slammed against a large boulder, bringing her downward spiral to an abrupt halt. In spite of the searing pain, she clamped down on her jaw to keep from moaning.

Play dead, an inner voice warned.

Pete stopped at the top of the gorge and fired two more rounds. One hit the boulder that was flush against her cheek. She flinched at the near miss but lay still.

"It's me." His voice cut through the night. "I've had a setback." He mumbled something. Was he on his phone?

She kept her eyes closed and willed her body to remain still.

"Gotta find the keys. If the car runs, I'll get

to Mountain Crest in time. Otherwise, you'll have to pick me up."

Another pause. She feared he could hear the *thump-thump-thump* of her heart.

"The driver's dead. I'll dispose of her body later."

From the rustle of leaves and the sound of his footfalls, she knew he was walking away from the edge of the steep incline.

Relieved that playing dead had worked, she tried to sit up. Her head swirled, nausea washed over her and she collapsed onto the soggy Georgia red clay. The loamy scent filled her nostrils and made her stomach roil as she slipped into an ethereal place where no one could hurt her and where she didn't have to worry about a man with a gun.

A dog's bark drew her back to the cold Georgia night. She blinked her eyes open. An arc of light from a lantern revealed a Labrador retriever standing over her. He licked her face and gently nudged her shoulder.

Her heart nearly froze when a man—long legs, muscular build and strong hands—reached down to touch her forehead.

She jerked back. "No."

"Don't be afraid."

He wore a wide-brim hat, had dark hair that

curled around his ears and deep-set eyes that stared at her.

"I'm Matthias Overholt. From the blood on your shoulder, I see that you're hurt."

Lulled by the concern in his voice, Lily tried to sit up. Her head spun, and another wave of vertigo swept over her as she floated, once again, back into darkness.

Matthias stood in the guest room of his farmhouse and stared down at the young woman he had carried home. His mother, Fannie Overholt, *tsked* with concern and wrung her hands.

"What happened to her, Matthias?"

"Hopefully, she will tell us when she wakes."

His mother nodded. "At least her wound looks superficial. I'll apply a poultice before I bandage her shoulder and change her into dry clothing."

"The main road up the mountain is on the far side of the gorge. She might have been in a car accident before taking the fall."

"*Ack*, a vehicular accident does not end with what looks like a gunshot wound. More is underfoot." Fannie shooed him out of the guest bedroom. "Leave me to my work."

Matthias walked to the kitchen, grabbed his hat off the wall peg and settled it on his head as he left the house and stared into the night. He had wanted to downplay the seriousness of the woman's plight to his mother, but they'd both heard the gunshots and knew the shooter could still be in the area.

Duke sauntered toward him. "Hey, boy. Have you been keeping watch?" He scratched behind the dog's ears and then slapped his leg, inviting Duke to join him.

Together, they walked around the barn and other outbuildings, stopping at regular intervals to search the night. The *hoo-hoo-hoo* of the great horned owl sounded, along with the throaty croak of a few tree frogs that hadn't yet gone into hibernation. The moon peered through the clouds and provided enough light for Matthias to stare at the pastures and fields and watch for anything that seemed suspect. At last, satisfied no one was hiding in the shadows, he returned to the kitchen with Duke at his heels.

His mother was sitting at the table, a cup of hot coffee in hand and a worried look on her face. "We do not need trouble, Matthias."

"We do not," he agreed. "But we need to help this woman who has stumbled onto our property. She is a child of *Gott*, *Mamm*, and we will welcome her as we would any visitor."

His *mamm* raised her brow. "For all we know, she could be running from the law."

Matthias shook his head. "Is this my sweet mother talking such nonsense?"

"Your mother realizes the lives of the *Englisch* are filled with strife. This woman may have secrets in her past that we do not want unlocked. Think of the twins."

"I hope Toby and Sarah learn the gift of hospitality is extended to all who come to our door."

"May I remind you that she did not come to our door? You found her on an outcrop of the gorge."

"Duke found her, and for that, I am grateful. Now go to bed and get some sleep. Morning will come soon, and then we can learn more about our houseguest."

"*Yah*, you are right." She glanced toward the small downstairs bedroom where the woman was sleeping. "But watch yourself, Matthias. Fancy women can turn a *gut* man's eye."

"No one is turning my eye, *Mamm*."

"Perhaps the widow Hershberger?"

He shook his head. "Not even the widow Hershberger, no matter how many pies and cakes she brings to our house."

"She is lonely, Matthias, and your Rachel died seven years ago. It is time."

"It is time for you to get some sleep."

She offered him a weak smile and climbed the stairs, leaving him to pour a cup of coffee and sit at the table. Duke dropped to the floor at his feet, and he rubbed the dog's ears.

"Seems we have a pre-Christmas visitor, Duke, thanks to you finding her tonight. Good job, boy."

The dog looked up at Matthias.

"You miss Rachel," he said. "I do too. More than my mother realizes. The Christmas season is always hard, *yah*, with the memories. Perhaps this year, *Gott* has brought us a special visitor to turn our thoughts from Christmases past."

An unusual but pleasant distraction, Matthias thought. Although, his mother was right. A fancy woman could turn a man's eye.

He let out a deep sigh as he stared at the guest room door. *What's your secret, lady, and why did you stumble into my life two weeks before Christmas?*

TWO

Lily woke with a start. Her head pounded, her mouth was dry as a wad of cotton and her shoulder ached as if a leather strap had rubbed her raw.

She blinked at the moonlight filtering through the navy blue curtain and moved her hand over the quilt that covered the bed. Rolling to her side, she threw off the covering, dropped her bare feet to the cold hardwood floor and fought off the urge to crawl back into bed and close her eyes to the confusion that played through her very troubled mind.

Seeing the wall pegs, small chest of drawers and ladder-back chair, she raised her brow. If she didn't know better, she'd have thought she was in an Amish house. But why and how she had gotten here alluded her.

The last she remembered was leaving Pinewood and driving along the mountain road. Pulling in a deep breath, she reached for the robe at the bottom of the bed, tied it around her waist and padded across the floor to the door.

Water. She needed a drink. She also needed answers to the questions that ricocheted through her head.

The hallway lay dark and quiet as she breathed in the scent of an oil lamp. She followed a hint of light that opened into a kitchen.

Spying the sink and faucet, she hurried past the small table bathed in shadow, turned on the spigot, pooled the cool liquid in her hands and drank deeply. With a twist of her fingers, she splashed water against her eyes and rubbed her hands across her pounding forehead, hoping to ease the tension that tightened her head and neck.

"How are you feeling?"

She startled at the words spoken behind her and turned abruptly to stare into the darkened corner where a large presence pulled himself upright. For half a heartbeat, she wanted to run back to the bedroom, bar the door and stand quaking in her bare feet.

Instead, she steeled her resolve, squared her shoulders and grimaced at the pain that radiated down her left side as she turned off the water.

"You surprised me," she admitted, wishing her voice were stronger and more assertive. Whoever the man was, she hoped he was friend not foe.

"I'm Matthias Overholt. We met last night halfway down the gorge."

A memory of a wagging tail and the friendly pup who had nudged her out of her lethargy returned. As if her thoughts had a power of their own, a dog lumbered toward her.

"Duke found you." The man's deep voice held a soothing resonance, and the sweet dog's friendly greeting as he waited for a pat calmed her fears even more.

She dried her hands on a nearby towel and bent to rub behind the dog's ears. "I remember you, Duke."

A slideshow of still shots flashed through her mind: the white sedan angled into a ditch, the man with a duffel bag, his upset and the click of the revolver pointed at her head.

She shivered as her memory returned full force. "A man aimed a gun at me and fired. The bullet grazed my flesh." She touched her shoulder and felt the bandage through the flannel robe and gown. "I... I lost my balance and tumbled down a sharp incline."

"The gorge is at the far side of my farm, some distance from here." Matthias stepped from the shadows. He was big and broad with an angular face and crystal-blue eyes.

"I heard gunshots," he continued. "Duke and I set out to find what had happened."

"I'm grateful, Mr. Over—" She tried to recall his full name.

"Matthias Overholt. And you are?"

"Lily Hudson." She wrapped her arms around her waist. "Thank you for saving me."

He nodded to the dog who had dropped to the floor at Lily's feet. "Duke's the one who deserves the thanks. I just followed his lead."

Matthias pointed to the aluminum coffeepot warming on the rear of the wood-burning stove. "It's early, but perhaps a cup of coffee would be *gut*?"

She nodded. "Thank you."

"You're from this area?"

"I live an hour south of Pinewood, which means a two-hour drive from Sunview."

"Yet you were heading up the mountain late last night."

She let out the breath she had been holding and made a decision to trust the muscular Amish man, who had more than likely saved her from a dangerous night in the wild. "I'll take that cup of coffee," she said, hoping to remind him of his offer.

He motioned her toward the table. "Please, sit. Perhaps you would like a slice of bread and jam as well?"

She rubbed her hand over her empty stomach, realizing it had been far too long since yesterday's lunch. "Bread and jam would be wonderful."

Working quickly, Matthias poured coffee into a cup and brought it along with a basket of sliced bread to the table. He retraced his steps and returned with butter and jam.

"I'll join you." He slipped into the chair at the head of the table.

She reached for a slice of bread, slathered it with butter and covered it with fruit preserves. Strawberry, her favorite. He did the same.

"Mmm," she hummed as she savored the first bite.

"My mother will appreciate your approval."

A hazy memory of an Amish woman helping her into bed floated through her mind.

"*Mamm* likes to feed people, including me and my children," Matthias continued.

Children?

"You're married?" she asked and regretted the disappointment she heard in her voice.

"I'm a widower. My wife, Rachel, died seven years ago when the twins were born."

Lily's heart broke at the pain that flashed momentarily from his gaze. "I'm sorry for your loss."

"Some say it was *Gott*'s will."

"Your children are seven?"

He nodded. "Toby and Sarah. You will meet

them soon. They are early birds, as the *Englisch* say."

Englisch. She forgot she was the outsider here. What else did they call the non-Amish? *Fancy?*

Glancing down at the flannel robe tied around her waist, she felt plain, very plain, not in the Amish way, but certainly not fancy either. She finished the slice of bread, wiped her mouth on the napkin, reached for the coffee and took a sip. Strong and black, the way she liked it.

"We were talking about last night," he said, returning to the subject she wanted to forget.

Lily glanced again at the man with the warm gaze, somewhat controlled beard and piercing blue eyes. She stared at him for a very long moment, until she realized she was making a spectacle of herself.

Trying to cover her embarrassment, she said the first thing that came to mind. "I run a local taxi business in Pinewood and sell crafts at weekend fairs."

He nodded in approval. "You are very industrious."

For some reason, she wanted to share more about the reality of her life. "Crafts don't bring in a lot of money."

Again, he nodded. "But the taxi business does?"

She shrugged. "At times. The small college in town keeps me busy."

"So last night you were giving college students a ride?"

"Hardly." She explained about the unexpected request to transport a motorist in need.

"A few folks in town work for rideshare companies, but it's doubtful anyone would have responded. I couldn't leave him stranded, although in hindsight, I regret my attempt to help."

Matthias listened attentively as she explained about the man's phone call to Bob and a second call to someone he was scheduled to meet. "He wanted to go farther up the mountain, but I agreed to take him to the motel in Sunview."

"Which was not to his liking?"

"Evidently not." She glanced down at the table for a long moment before adding, "A news flash came on the radio about a stolen white sedan. That's the color of the car in the ditch."

"Did he think you suspected him of being the car thief?"

She shrugged. "I don't know what he was thinking. All I know is that he drew a weapon and told me to pull off on a dirt road." She rubbed the rim of the coffee cup. "Perhaps I've read too many suspense novels, but I knew he wanted to get rid of me and take my car. So I crashed into a tree, grabbed my keys and ran for my life."

With a heavy sigh, she shook her head. "The

problem is I dropped the keys. I tried to find them, until Pete started closing in—"

"And he had a gun?"

"A gun and a rifle, but I'm a fast runner."

"I'm sure you are." Matthias tilted his head. "So who is this Pete?"

"That's what I'd like to know."

"There's a sheriff in Sunview."

Her stomach tightened. "Do you know the sheriff's name?"

"Granger. Doug Granger. He's been our chief law enforcement officer for more than a decade."

She recognized the name. "Sheriff Granger needs to retire."

Matthias stared at her, his eyes full of questions. "You know him?"

Unwilling to reveal anything about her past, she scooted back from the table and then stood and carried her plate and cup to the sink. "I've taken too much of your time. As soon as I find my clothes, I'll change and be on my way."

"Do you plan to walk to town?"

"Pardon?"

"What about your car?"

"I'll search for the keys." She bit her bottom lip. "Although I don't know what I'll do if Pete was able to hot-wire the ignition."

"That's a little more difficult these days."

"You know about cars?"

"My uncle moonlighted as a mechanic to make extra money. He taught me a lot."

"But you're Amish."

Matthias chuckled. "The Amish use engines. They just don't drive motor vehicles."

"Thanks for the clarification." She pointed to the sink. "I didn't expect running water."

"Different districts follow different rules. We use a gravity water tank system."

Glancing down at the flannel robe brought another question to mind. "And my clothing?"

He nodded toward the hallway. "Check the last door on the right. My children will be up in an hour or so. We'll have breakfast then."

Without further explanation, Matthias rose from the table, grabbed his hat and headed outside along with Duke, leaving Lily to stare after both of them for a long moment. She was never one to pray, but she said a quick thank-you that Matthias and his dog had found her and then removed the rest of the dishes from the table, washed them in the sink and placed them in the strainer to dry.

If the Overholts had a bathroom, she'd take a shower, but she doubted indoor plumbing included heated bath water. Still, she headed down the hall, opened the door Matthias had mentioned and was relieved to see a sink, toilet and shower.

Her clothes hung over the shower rack. A propane space heater ran nearby. The mud and blood had been washed away, and although the slacks and sweater were still slightly damp, they were clean and wearable. A thick terrycloth towel and a new package of toiletries sat on a nearby stand, for which she was grateful.

The credit card she kept in the pocket of her jeans as well as a few bills and a handful of change lay on a small table. Under the cash, she found the letter she had received a few days ago from her old friend Betsy.

The older Amish woman who had helped her last night must have placed the items on the table for safekeeping. Lily unfolded the letter and glanced at Betsy's neat cursive handwriting.

It's been five years, yet the rumors continue to circulate. You need to come back to Sunview, Lily, to clear your mother's name.

More than anything, Lily wanted to return to her cabin and forget what had happened five years ago as well as the events of last night. She kept thinking about Mr. Peterson and his late-night meeting in Mountain Crest. She also thought about the pistol he had brandished and the rifle in his duffel.

Call it her civic duty, but she had to let someone other than Matthias know that a gunman was on the loose. After everything that had happened in her youth, she couldn't let anyone in Sunview think she or anyone else in her family was responsible for another crime.

Betsy was right. She needed to clear her mother's name, and she needed to let the sheriff track down Peterson and bring him to justice. Concerned as she was about Peterson, she was also concerned about coming face-to-face with Sheriff Doug Granger again.

Matthias hauled feed to a distant pasture and filled the troughs with water, all while his thoughts were on Lily and the story she had shared this morning. The Amish took care of their own in most cases, and if what Lily had told him was true—and he had no reason to think she was prevaricating or embellishing the truth—someone in law enforcement needed to be told about the armed man.

His mother, who often spoke her mind, would tell Lily to ignore law enforcement and head home relieved she hadn't been more seriously injured. But his mother, for all her willingness to forgive and forget, still struggled with Sheriff Granger and the mistakes he had made in his past.

The logic of his mother's thinking surprised

him at times. She enjoyed having visitors in the house, and even though she had cautioned him about *Englisch* women, he wouldn't be surprised if she invited Lily to stay with them a few more days until her shoulder had fully healed.

The Christmas festival was fast approaching, and his mother would be the first to admit that an extra pair of hands could be put to good use. As much as they could use Lily's help, Matthias knew having her in the house would upset the status quo. No doubt, she would be a distraction, although a pretty distraction. He smiled to himself. Knowing Lily would join them for breakfast made him eager to complete the morning chores.

His mother stood at the stove when he entered the house. The smell of biscuits permeated the kitchen, along with the slices of ham in the skillet and the scrambled eggs warming. A pot of coffee sat on the back of the stove. After hauling feed to the livestock, he was ready for breakfast even after the bread and jam he had shared with Lily.

"You have seen our guest?" he asked his mother.

"She said her name is Lily Hudson, and in spite of the injury to her shoulder, she insisted on setting the table."

He glanced at the lined-up china plates, coffee cups and saucers, silverware and cloth napkins. Even his *mamm* could not set such a fine table.

His mother gave a satisfied nod. "Lily knows her way around the kitchen and is eager to help. For an *Englischer*, this is a welcome change."

"Yet you claim Natalie Keeper works harder than any woman you know."

"*Yah*, but she has the Christmas Lodge to run and the festival each year." His mother put her hand on her hip and paused for a moment with lips pursed before adding, "As hard as Natalie works, someone in her family tree must surely be Amish."

Matthias almost laughed at his mother's skewed thought process. "I doubt that, but we have many *Englischer* friends who are industrious. You should get over your prejudice."

"*Ack!* It is not prejudice. It is reality. Now, fetch the children. I woke them earlier, but they are slow this morning getting ready for school. Toby should have been helping you with the chores, and Sarah was needed in the kitchen."

"They are still young, but I'll hurry them along."

"You coddle them, Matthias."

His mother's admonition rolled over him as he climbed the stairs and thought back to his happiness the night of their births. Less than forty-eight hours later, Rachel was gone, and he was left to care for two babies without the help of his beautiful wife. The pain of her death washed over him again. *Yah*, he coddled the twins and protected them because he couldn't bear to think of ever losing someone else he loved.

He knocked on both their bedroom doors and peered in to see their beds neatly made and nightclothes tucked under their pillows.

"Good morning, my sweet children."

"Datt." Sarah ran to the doorway to hug him, and Toby joined them there.

Matthias never tired of their affectionate and enthusiastic greetings. He drew them close and kissed their cheeks, always amazed at how much they resembled their mother.

"Your grandmother has breakfast ready. We have a guest this morning. A nice lady who will stay with us for a day or two."

"Mammi said her name is Lily Hudson, but I can call her Miss Lily. Is she pretty?"

"Inner beauty is what's important, Sarah. Now hurry downstairs and see if *Mammi* needs help."

He looked at Toby's disheveled mane. "Come here, son. Let's comb your hair."

"I already did."

Matthias noted the cowlick at his crown that stood straight up. He grabbed a hairbrush off the dresser and smoothed the wayward tuft of hair into place. "Now you are ready for school."

Toby followed Matthias downstairs. Lily stood at the counter, pouring a cup of coffee. She glanced up when the boy charged toward the kitchen table.

"You must be Toby," she said with an endearing smile.

His son stopped short. The boy's eyes widened, and a rosy hue colored his cheeks. He seemed genuinely surprised by the sight of the pretty lady.

Matthias had to admit he was surprised too. He thought of the dirt-smudged face, matted hair and muddy clothing from last night and could hardly believe the woman standing before him was the same disheveled stray Duke had found and he had carried home. Her golden hair was neatly combed, and her face had been scrubbed and was now tinged with a healthy glow. The poultice his mother had applied to her shoulder must have worked by the way she effortlessly handled the coffeepot.

"*Guder mariye*, Matthias." She held out a filled cup. "You are ready for coffee, *yah*?"

"You know how to say *good morning* in Pennsylvania Dutch?" He accepted the cup and glanced at his *mamm*, who nodded.

"Your mother was kind enough to teach me a few words."

Her smile and the way she flattered his mother warmed Matthias's heart. Fannie Overholt had her own opinions about the *Englisch*, especially anyone who didn't pull his or her fair share of the daily load. From all appearances, Lily had gotten off to a good start.

Sarah tugged on their houseguest's arm. "*Mammi* said you are staying for a day or two."

"*Mammi*? Is what you call your grandma?" Lily asked.

"*Yah*, my grandmother."

Lily looked at the older woman.

"Call me Fannie." His mother's smile made Matthias think that she too seemed taken by their guest.

Once again, Sarah grabbed Lily's arm. "Do you like to play jacks?"

"I do, but be forewarned." Lily's eyes twinkled. "I'm very good at jacks."

"*Gut,*" Matthias's mother corrected. "The Amish say *gut*."

"*Danki*, Fannie." Lily nodded to his mother and then turned back to Sarah and leaned closer. "Be forewarned that I am very *gut* at jacks."

His daughter giggled. "We will play after school."

"Deal." Lily raised her hand. "High five?"

Sarah slapped the woman's hand. "*Yah*, it's a deal."

Matthias raised his brow. "Since when did my daughter learn to high five?"

"At school, of course, *Datt*."

He had to chuckle. "Of course."

Lily turned to Toby. "What about Amish boys? Do they play jacks?"

He shrugged. "Sometimes, but I like pick-up sticks."

"That's another favorite game of mine. Maybe we'll have time to play that as well."

Toby smiled, his cheeks still flushed. "Maybe."

"Sit, sit." His mother shooed them to the table. "Lily, take the chair next to me."

"May I help you serve?" Lily asked.

"*Yah*, this would be *gut*." His mother filled the plates, and Lily placed them in front of the hungry children before serving Matthias. Finally, the two women carried their plates to the table.

Lily watched Matthias and followed his lead by bowing her head. When he glanced up, she smiled, causing his neck to warm.

"Where's Duke this morning?" She spread the cloth napkin over her lap and reached for her fork.

"Outside, where dogs belong," his mother said with a definitive nod. "Last night, he slept in the kitchen. Matthias spoils him."

"You spoil him too, *Mammi*," Toby chimed in, "when you give him scraps from the table."

Matthias laughed. "Toby Overholt, you see too much and say too much as well."

He looked at the wall clock. "Eat, children, so you can get to school on time." He turned to his mother. "If you don't mind, *Mamm*, would you take them in the buggy? I want to help Lily with her car."

Matthias didn't want the children walking to school when the man who'd accosted Lily might still be in the area. His mother nodded knowingly, as if she too realized danger could be lurking nearby. He glanced at Lily, and the lightheartedness she had exuded earlier evaporated. The three adults were careful about what they said in front of the twins, but there was no doubt all of them were concerned about not only Lily's safety, but also the children's.

After finishing breakfast, Toby and Sarah hugged him, waved goodbye to Lily and then grabbed their book bags and lunch boxes and hurried outside.

Lily cleared the table.

His mother stopped her. "I will wash the dishes when I return home."

"Are you sure I can't help?"

"Another time. You and Matthias have something to do, *yah*?"

His mother's earlier concern about having an *Englisch* houseguest seemed to have disappeared completely, for which he was glad. Although how could his mother not approve of someone so willing to help?

"I need to see if my car is where I left it last night," Lily said as she rinsed her hands and dried them.

"We will go together to find your keys," Matthias insisted.

"Are you sure?"

He held up his hand and nodded. "It is settled."

"Be careful," his mother warned.

"Tell Toby and Sarah that someone will pick them up after school. Until we learn more about the man last night, we must be cautious."

"I'm so sorry." Lily frowned. "I've caused you problems."

"You are not the problem," he told her. "The man who attacked you is."

"But I've brought danger to you and your family."

Matthias realized the truth of her statement. Although he was concerned about the man from last night, he was more worried about the impact Lily might have on his family. He could tell from the way his children had responded to Lily that she brought a freshness to their home that had been lacking. The twins were impressionable and gave their hearts so easily—too easily. He didn't want them hurt either by the man who had attacked Lily or by the sweet visitor who would make them realize what they'd missed due to Rachel's passing.

Although Matthias didn't want to admit it, Lily posed a problem to him as well. For seven years, he had resisted the attention of Amish women. Now, after just a few hours, he seemed as taken as Toby with their houseguest. And she wasn't even Amish.

THREE

Lily had trouble keeping up with Matthias's long strides as they followed the lengthy path to the gorge. Their hike took time, but when they finally neared the edge, Lily stopped to catch her breath and glanced at the steep incline. Landing on the ledge halfway down the drop-off had, more than likely, saved her life.

She shivered and rubbed her hands together. Matthias touched her arm. "Are you okay?"

"Just thinking of what could have happened." She stared into his blue eyes. "Thank you again for rescuing me."

"I told you, Duke deserves the praise." He glanced at the path they had just traversed and smiled. "Looks like somebody wants to join us."

Duke ran toward them. At the last moment, he dashed off to chase a squirrel that rummaged in the underbrush.

Lily smiled at his antics. "I'm grateful to both of you."

"Duke can catch up to us later." Matthias pointed to an adjoining path and motioned her forward. "The road's not quite as difficult to navigate if we go this way."

Just as he had said, they arrived at the paved roadway within a quarter of an hour. Lily let out a sigh of relief when she spied her car.

"The dent in your front bumper needs to be hammered out, but that shouldn't take too long. We'll check under the hood later, once we find the keys. Where did you drop them?"

"Not far from here." Lily glanced around, trying to orient herself. "I pulled them from the ignition and leaped from the car. Then I started running."

Matthias pointed to an area ahead. "You went this way, perhaps?"

"Maybe." She shrugged. "It was dark. I can't be sure."

He forged into the undergrowth, kicked at piles of leaves and raked his hands through some of the thicker mounds of pine straw.

"I'll look in this direction." Lily headed to where a narrow path twisted deeper into the woods. She couldn't be certain whether she had passed this way last night, but by separating, she and Matthias could cover more territory.

The floor of the forest was dense with under-brush, which made the search slow and laborious. She glanced up every few minutes to get her bearings before starting off again.

Discouraged by her lack of success, she was ready to retrace her steps when a twig snapped on the path ahead. Realizing Matthias must have circled around to where she was, she scurried forward.

Another twig snapped.

"Matthias?"

She pushed on, determined to catch up to him. He was headed to the gorge and seemed to be moving at a fast pace. Maybe he had found her keys and was looking for her.

Breaking out of the densely forested area, she glanced at the edge of the steep incline but saw no one.

Strange. She *had* heard twigs snap.

Turning, she retraced her steps. The memory of last night washed over her, and she shivered as the forest seemed to close in around her.

Footsteps sounded behind her. She glanced over her shoulder and cocked her ear. "Matthias?"

Turning back to the path, she tried to calm her heart.

More footsteps.

She had an eerie feeling that something sinister was nearby, and whether the footsteps belonged to Matthias or not, she wanted to get back to her car.

Branches cracked underfoot, and leaves crunched as the person following her drew ever closer.

She ran through a thick stand of trees. From out of nowhere, a hand grabbed her wounded shoulder. Pain ricocheted up her neck and down her spine. She jerked free, but her attacker grabbed her again and shoved her to the ground. Pain, even more severe, cut through her. She rolled to her back.

A man stood over her. He wore a military-style stocking cap, black slacks and a camouflage jacket.

Pete!

"I thought you were dead and came back to bury your body." His voice was low and menacing.

He lunged for her, but she rolled away, scrambled to her feet and dove deeper into the forest.

"Why you—" Pete chased after her. "You won't get away from me. I'll find you, and I'll kill you."

She pushed a large tree branch back and let it swing free once she had passed. It crashed into him, throwing him off balance. He dropped to his knees, shook his head and crawled to his feet.

Hurrying on, she was confused about which direction to go. She needed to get to the main road. Was she headed back to the gorge?

Her lungs burned, and she gasped for air.

Hearing him close in again, she glanced back, and her heart nearly stopped when she saw the raised pistol aimed directly at her. She lunged behind a boulder. A round hit the rock and shards of granite flew into the air.

Gathering her courage, she angled deeper into the woods and ran as fast as she could. Another round *hissed* past her, then one more shattered the bark on a nearby tree.

Through the underbrush, she spied her car.

A hand grabbed her arm. A second hand covered her mouth and pulled her flush against a rock-hard chest.

She struggled to free herself.

"Lily," he whispered.

Her knees went weak. "Matthias."

"Shhh." His breath played along her neck.

Pete's voice sounded nearby. "I'm gonna kill you."

Duke raced past them, growling. He headed straight toward the man in camo and nipped at his legs.

"Get outta here, dog. No! Stop it."

A gunshot rang out. Lily gasped and was overcome with relief when she saw Duke chasing after the fleeing attacker. Duke's barking continued until a car engine started and tires screeched on the road, heading up the mountain.

Lily lingered for a moment more in Matthias's arms before she left the warmth of his embrace. He seemed equally as confused by their closeness as she was.

Duke raced back and rubbed against her leg. She bent to pet him. "Looks like Duke came to my rescue once again."

Matthias pointed to something nearly buried in the pine straw.

Lily glanced down and smiled. "My keys!"

Matthias picked them up, took her arm and motioned her toward her car. "Let's leave before Pete returns to do more harm. My farm is a distance from here and on one of the back roads. It is doubtful the man will search for you there, but we must still be careful."

Knowing Pete could be in the area made Lily even more anxious. As they hurried to her car, his words kept playing over in her mind.

I'll find you, and I'll kill you.

Matthias sat in the passenger seat, and Duke rode in the back as Lily drove along the roads that eventually led to the farm. He opened the barn door and showed her where to park her car to keep it out of sight. Opening the rear door to let Duke out, Matthias noticed something under the seat.

He reached for the small object and held it up to Lily. "Is this your flash drive?"

Lily looked surprised. "You know about computers?"

"I worked at the local sawmill as a teen and learned how to use computers there so I could order supplies."

"You called me industrious last night. Seems I could say the same about you."

"The Amish are known for their *gut* work ethic."

"And your love of family, which I admire." She glanced at his worktable and then stepped toward the hickory rocking chair he was making.

Lily ran her hand over the smooth arm of the chair. A small chest of drawers he was building for his mother sat nearby. Glancing back at him, Lily smiled.

"Looks like you learned more than computers at the sawmill. The furniture is lovely, Matthias."

He shrugged off the compliment. "Woodworking keeps me busy, especially when the fields lie dormant in the winter."

"You should sell the furniture you make at the local fairs."

"I do sometimes."

She stared at him for a long moment and then reached for the flash drive he held out to her.

"It's not mine," she said, "but it could belong

to Pete. He rummaged around in his backpack for a long time trying to find his second phone."

"The guy had two phones?"

"Strange, right? One was a smartphone, but the other one was a cheap prepaid model."

"You mean the type sold in drugstores and big-box stores?"

"That's what it looked like to me. Supposedly, they're hard to trace."

Matthias nodded. "I read about them in one of the handyman magazines. They're sometimes called burner phones because they're inexpensive and don't leave a trail."

"Pete used his cheap phone to call someone about his meeting in Mountain Crest, but he used his smartphone to call Bob, the friend who was supposed to contact a towing service."

She motioned Matthias to the rear of her car. "We can use my laptop to see what's on the flash drive. It's in my trunk, along with my purse and an overnight bag."

"You were planning to take a trip?"

A smile graced her lips. "I like to be prepared for any contingency. Locking my purse and laptop in the trunk keeps them secure. The overnight bag is in case I decide to visit my aunt and spend the night."

"Your aunt lives around here?"

"In Pinewood. She takes care of my mom."

"Your mother is infirm?"

"She's..." Lily thought for a moment and shrugged. "She gets confused."

Lily opened the trunk and grabbed her purse. Matthias noticed the assortment of craft items neatly arranged in plastic containers.

"You mentioned craft fairs," he said. "From the number of items in your trunk, it looks like you're running a business out of the back of your car."

"I had a table at an event in Boulder Bluff last weekend," Lily explained. "Sales weren't good, and I ended up with a lot of remaining merchandise."

Matthias eyed the various Christmas ornaments, wreaths, tree skirts and stockings. "You're very talented, Lily."

Her cheeks pinked. "I work on my crafts when the taxi business is slow. Kind of like you with the woodworking." She pointed to her laptop. "My computer is behind that box of ornaments."

He moved the storage container aside and placed her laptop on his workbench.

"Let's see what's on Pete's flash drive." Lily booted up her computer, typed in her password and inserted the flash drive into the URL port. A list of three files appeared on the screen.

Matthias stared at the screen. "Open the most

recently saved file, and we'll see what he's been up to."

"Here's one saved last week titled *Brochure*." Lily double-clicked on the file.

"Did Pete mention the Christmas Lodge?" Matthias asked as the file opened.

"What do you mean?"

He pointed to a photo on the screen that showcased a grand hotel set on a hillside in front of a lake. A wide porch wrapped around the front of the wooden four-story structure. Rocking chairs lined the porch, along with twinkling lights, greenery and Christmas wreaths.

She inhaled deeply. "The Christmas Lodge."

"You know about it?"

Lily glanced up. "My mother worked there when I was a kid."

Matthias stared at her. "So you grew up in this area?" Was that why she had reacted to Sheriff Granger's name?

"My mother and I left town a few days before the Christmas break of my senior year in high school." She turned back to the screen. "Last night, Pete didn't seem to know anything about the lodge."

"Looks like he does."

Lily clicked on the photo gallery section and shots of the warm and welcoming reception area, dining room and various guest rooms filled the screen, followed by pictures of the Christmas festival. A large banner across the top of the page read The Keepers Keep Christmas Alive 365 Days a Year!

More photos showed some of the items usually up for sale at the Christmas Store as well as during the festival—nativity scenes, inflatable snowmen, even a full-size sleigh filled with Christmas quilts.

Lily pulled up a new page. "Here's a layout of the rooms so guests can decide where they want to stay."

"What's on the last page?" he asked.

She flipped to the end of the e-brochure. "The back page shows the stage by the lake set up for the entertainment the night of the festival. Clay Lambert's performing this year."

"You probably went to school with him."

She smiled. "Actually, I did. He's a nice guy, and his mom was always super sweet."

After closing the brochure, she clicked on the next file. "That's strange."

A series of straight lines appeared on a white background. All the lines converged at one central point.

"What do you think that is?" he asked.

"No clue," Lily said. "There's one more file that was loaded last week."

The file opened. Matthias peered at the screen

and read the invoice. *"Payment will be divided into two sums. Half upon arrival and half after the job is done."*

He pursed his lips. "Evidently, Pete was hired to do some type of job."

"I'll save the files to my computer to make sure we have them in case something happens to the flash drive."

"If you've got a phone, you might want to take a screen shot of the graphic as well as the invoice."

After tapping a few keys on her computer and phone, she nodded. "Done."

As she continued to stare at the files, her face clouded.

"Is something wrong?" he asked.

"Maybe I'm jumping to the wrong conclusion—" Lily's voice was tight with emotion "—but I keep thinking about the rifle in his duffel bag. I thought he planned to hunt game, but what if—" She pulled in a weak breath. "What if the prey he's hunting is human? If so, that means there's a killer on the loose, and I drove him to Sunview."

"No matter why Pete came to this area, you're not responsible for his actions."

"You don't understand how *Englisch* folks think, Matthias. If they're looking for someone to blame, they'll have no problem believing a lie." Her mouth was drawn. "I could never forgive myself if someone else dies."

Someone else?

Matthias's gut tightened. What was Lily trying to tell him? Had someone died previously, and if so, had Lily been involved?

FOUR

Lily didn't want to reveal the painful story of her past, but Matthias and Fannie deserved to know the truth about the stranger they had welcomed into their home.

"I need to tell you something," she said to Matthias after he and Lily returned to the kitchen. "Your mother needs to hear what I have to say, too."

Matthias looked perplexed, and no wonder. His life had been peaceful and nonviolent until last night when she had shown up. His concern about the gunshots he had heard had sent him searching in the night and, thankfully for her, he and Duke had found her.

"Is something wrong?" Fannie asked as she hurried downstairs. "I heard a vehicle in the driveway." She glanced at Lily. "You found your car?"

Lily nodded. "But we also found the man who chased after me last night." She stooped down and patted Duke, who had scurried inside with them. "Duke frightened him away."

"This man with a gun is afraid of Duke?" Fannie's brow raised.

"Perhaps he had a bad experience with dogs in the past. Whatever the reason, it worked to our advantage and sent him fleeing."

Fannie's gaze narrowed. "But your face is drawn, so there is something else you need to tell us."

Lily motioned both of them to the table. "This might take a bit of time, so we should probably sit down."

"I'll pour coffee." Attentive to the needs of others, Fannie removed three cups from the cupboard and filled them with coffee. After placing them on the table, she slipped into her seat and lifted the cup to her lips. "Coffee helps me focus when difficult situations need to be discussed."

Lily took a sip from her cup as well. Fannie was right. This discussion would be difficult.

After returning the cup to the table, Lily removed Betsy's letter from her pocket and unfolded the paper.

"I'm not sure if you read the letter, Fannie, when you helped me into bed last night, but it's from an old friend."

"I saw only that it was a folded piece of paper. What was written there was not for my eyes, unless you requested that I read what the note contained."

"Thank you for respecting my privacy, but it's time for me to explain a few things about my past."

She glanced at Matthias and offered him a weak smile. More than anything, she didn't want her generous host to think poorly of her.

He nodded as if to reassure her, which warmed her heart. She felt like Matthias was the type of man who looked for the good in people instead of the bad, and she hoped he would see her in a positive light.

Pulling in a deep breath, she started to share her story. "I lived in Sunview when I was a girl with my mother, Violet."

Fannie's eyes widened ever so slightly, which made Lily pause. "Did you want to say something?"

"Continue, dear. You have my attention."

"My mother worked in housekeeping at the Christmas Lodge. Occasionally, the owners would invite me to come with my mother for the day. Mr. and Mrs. Keeper's daughter, Noelle, was my age."

She splayed her hands. "The Christmas Lodge, as you know, is a distance from town, so Noelle rarely had playmates unless I visited. She and I would spend the day running across the landscaped lawns, wading in the lake or romping through the lodge in the various rooms that weren't occupied."

"You were close friends?" Matthias asked.

"As children, but in our high school years, our friendship waned. She was dating Sheriff Granger's son, Kevin. Most of our high school class thought he and Noelle would get married, yet—"

A lump formed in Lily's throat, and the words she wanted to say refused to be uttered.

Fannie leaned across the table and rubbed Lily's hand. "We know that Noelle was murdered." Her tone underscored the horror of that terrible tragedy.

Lily blinked back tears that stung her eyes. "I… I wasn't sure you'd heard about her death."

"*Ack*, the news spread quickly throughout the county, if not farther. You do not forget something like this." Fannie leaned closer. "But there is more you need to tell."

Fannie was right. There was more to tell. Not that Lily would mention her own reaction to Noelle's plight that night. She still regretted her inability to forgive her former friend and her parents for the accusation they had leveled against her mother. Glancing at Matthias, Lily saw compassion in his gaze. Pulling in a shallow breath, she continued.

"My mother liked her job at the lodge, and she received good reviews from her supervisor." She looked at Fannie and then back at Matthias. "You may know Mrs. Lambert. Her son is the singing star, Clay Lambert. At that time, she supervised the housekeeping department."

"*Yah*, we know her," Matthias said. "She works with the Amish vendors at the festival."

"A nice lady. She was always cordial and upbeat. Clay took after her and was so much nicer than his good friend, Kevin."

"Sheriff Granger's son?" Matthias asked.

Lily nodded. "The two guys were close and palled around a lot, but Kevin thought he was better than everyone else, whereas Clay was a friend to all, like his mother."

Fannie nodded, and Lily realized the sweet Amish woman could sense the struggle Lily had endured during her high school years.

"You were, perhaps, sweet on Clay when you were in school?" Fannie asked.

Lily could feel her cheeks warm. "You mean, did I have a crush on him?"

Fannie nodded. "That is what I meant."

"Not a crush, but Clay was always nice and took the time to talk to me, which I appreciated. As you can imagine, my mother didn't make much money. I tried to help by working at the City Café."

She glanced at Matthias. "Is the restaurant still open?"

"*Yah*, it does a *gut* business."

"Between what I made and my mother's salary, we managed. We rented a small two-bedroom house located on the other side of the train tracks some distance from town."

Lily paused as the memory of always being the outsider returned anew.

Once again, Fannie patted her hand. "Is it necessary that you tell us this, Lily? I see the pain on your face."

"It is necessary." Lily pulled in a breath and steeled her shoulders, knowing she had to continue. "Just before the start of the Christmas school break, Mrs. Keeper called my mother into her office and accused my mother of stealing money from her desk."

She glanced at Matthias. "The accusation was false, but my mother was fired, and it crushed her. She liked working at the lodge and thought Mrs. Keeper appreciated having her on the payroll."

"Something else was involved, perhaps?" he asked.

Lily rubbed her hands together. "My mother had a relationship with the sheriff."

"Sheriff Doug Granger?" Matthias asked.

"That's right." Lily nodded. "He promised my mother that he would leave his wife and marry her, but he lied. The day she was fired, he broke off their relationship. Mother was brokenhearted and wanted to leave town and never see him again. She had dated other men in the past and had been hurt by them, but she thought Sheriff Granger was different."

Fannie harrumphed. "I have never trusted the sheriff."

"Mamm," Matthias cautioned his mother. "Let Lily finish."

"My mother wasn't the only one who was hurting," Lily continued. "I had planned to work full-time over the Christmas break to earn extra money, but my mother wanted to leave Sunview as soon as possible. She was embarrassed that she had been fired and was upset that the sheriff had broken off their relationship."

"Of course, we can understand the hurt your mother felt," Fannie said. "Even though her relationship with the sheriff was not according to *Gott*'s will."

"My mother saw things through a different lens. Her faith in God was weak, and she had a hard life. I doubt she realized the pain she was causing the sheriff's family, although the sheriff was the one to instigate their relationship. He wooed my mother, and she believed the lies he told her. As a woman who longed to be loved, she was drawn to him."

"And you, dear?" Fannie asked.

"I struggled with my mother's choices. Once news of their relationship got out, the few kids who had been nice to me wouldn't even acknowledge me at school." Lily touched the letter she had placed on the table. "Except for Betsy. She remained a friend, although with my studies and work schedule, we rarely got together outside of school."

"A friend is always a blessing."

Lily appreciated Fannie's understanding.

"But how does all of this have bearing on Noelle Keeper's death?" Matthias asked.

Lily rubbed her hand over the table's smooth surface and wished she could smooth over the truth of the past as easily. The richness of the wood and the detail in the craftsmanship made her realize Matthias had more than likely made the table. Perhaps for his wife when they were first married.

She sighed again, and for a fleeting moment, she wondered why she was sharing her story with these two wonderful people. She didn't know if they would understand how chaotic her life had been and the pain she had endured.

Again, she looked at Matthias and realized he, too, carried the burden of his wife's death. He was a single man raising his sweet twins without the help of his wife. He'd had his own struggles, so perhaps he could understand the reality of her life.

"My mother picked me up at work the night the sheriff ended their relationship. She told me on the way home that we were leaving Sunview. I didn't want to move, but I couldn't convince her otherwise."

Her fingers played over the tabletop. "As we crossed the railroad tracks and got closer to our house, we noticed a girl walking alone some distance from the road. My mother wanted to stop and offer her a ride. The night was cold. There was snow on the ground, and that area of the road was dark."

"Did you recognize her?" Matthias asked.

"I recognized her pretty wool coat and the stocking cap she wore. It was Noelle Keeper."

"Your mother stopped the car," Matthias said, "but I have a sinking feeling that Noelle didn't accept the ride."

Lily wouldn't share all the details about that night and still regretted the hateful feelings that had welled up within her. "Noelle insisted she was meeting someone in a clearing just ahead. A car drove by and saw us talking to her. She became agitated and assured us she would be fine."

"So you went home," Fannie said.

"But only after my mother begged Noelle to

let us drive her. She said her parents knew where she was, and they planned to pick her up in a few minutes. As you can imagine, my mother didn't want to see the Keepers. Noelle convinced both of us that she was safe and would soon be with her family."

Lily bit her lip. "Unfortunately, that was a mistake we can never correct."

"Her body was found the next day?" Fannie asked.

"One of the deputies knocked on our door. He questioned us, then he called his office to talk to Sheriff Granger, after which he informed my mother that the sheriff wanted her to leave town as soon as possible. My mother wasn't thinking of her own well-being. She was thinking only of another rejection from Sheriff Granger."

"So you left Sunview?" Matthias stated.

"Later that night. We didn't have much, but packing our things and closing the house took longer than we expected. We learned that rumors had started circulating through town by that afternoon. The person who had driven by us on the dark road said my mother was the last person to see Noelle alive. From there, it was easy for people to wonder if my mother was the killer."

"Which is why you never returned to Sunview?"

Lily nodded. "That's right. I never wanted to come back."

Matthias pointed to the folded paper on the table. "But your friend's letter changed your mind?"

"She said the rumors have intensified over the last few weeks. The day of the festival will be exactly five years since Noelle was killed. Betsy said I need to return to clear my mother's name."

"Did she suggest how you could do that?"

"Only that I need to confront some of the people who continue to talk about my mother's involvement."

"People from your high school class?"

"Mainly Kevin Granger. I made reservations at the B and B in town starting today and running through the festival. Betsy's right. I can't let people believe the lies about my mother. Perhaps I can talk to Clay Lambert and explain what happened. He might be able to convince Kevin that the rumors need to end. Clay's mother might help as well."

"And the Keepers?" Fannie asked.

Lily sighed. "I'm not sure I can face them, knowing that they accused my mother of theft and then fired her. I don't know if they thought my mother was involved in their daughter's death, but whether they did or not, I need to clear her name and expose the person who killed Noelle."

"The sheriff has not been able to do so," Fannie said.

"Betsy said his investigation wasn't very thorough. Perhaps I can uncover new information."

"After five years, that seems unlikely," Matthias reasoned.

"But I have to try."

Fannie again patted Lily's hand. "I am certain Matthias would do the same if I were unjustly accused of wrongdoing." She glanced at her son and then back at Lily. "How can we help?"

Relief fluttered over Lily. She hadn't expected Matthias and his mother to be so understanding.

"You've done so much already," Lily said. "I can't involve your family or do anything to bring danger to either of you or to the children."

She glanced around the kitchen and offered them a weak smile. "As soon as I gather my things, I'll drive to town and will stay at least a couple days at the B and B."

"But what about Peterson?" Matthias asked.

"I'm not going to let him deter me from correcting the rumors about my mother. I plan to contact Betsy. She'll help me."

"And Sheriff Granger? Will you talk to him?"

She swallowed hard. "I have to tell him what happened last night so he and his deputies will be on the lookout for Peterson. I'm hoping they'll arrest him and get him off the streets."

Matthias tapped the table for emphasis. "It is too dangerous for you to stay in town."

"I have to, Matthias."

"Stay here instead."

"And bring danger to your family? I can't do that."

"My property is far from Mountain Road, and the gorge separates my land from other Amish farms that are closer to where you left your car. If Pete suspects you found refuge in the area, he would search along the main road, never suspecting you would have stumbled onto an Amish farm such a distance from the gorge."

"I hope you're right, but I need to go to town. If Sunview Garage is still open, I'll have the mechanic check my car before I head down the mountain in the next day or two."

"We cannot talk you into staying here?" Fannie asked.

"Thank you for the offer, but it is better if I go."

"Yet if there is a problem in town, you will come back, *yah*?"

"I don't think there will be a problem, Fannie."

"I am meeting a man in town this afternoon," Matthias said. "After I talk to him, I'll stop by the B and B and ensure you're all right."

Lily was touched by his thoughtfulness. "I wouldn't want you to make a special trip to town for me, but if you're already there, I'd enjoy seeing you."

"What if Peterson is renting a room at the B and B?" he asked.

"I'll make certain no one fitting his description is staying there."

"I would feel better if you'd call ahead."

"Of course, I can do that prior to leaving, but right now I need to gather my things together."

She carried her cup to the sink and hurried into the guest room before Fannie or Matthias tried to convince her to stay with them for another night. Their concern for her safety touched her deeply. Remaining in this peaceful Amish setting would be wonderful, but she had to make good decisions when it came to their safety and the safety of Matthias's children.

She thought back to the years after leaving Sunview and her mother's steady cognitive decline. Eventually, they had moved in with Lily's aunt who still took care of her mother. Two years ago, Lily had struck out on her own. With her taxi business and sales at the various craft fairs, she had managed to make ends meet and also pay for her mother's medical needs. Lily would return to her *fancy* life, as Amish would call it, although deep down, she knew she didn't want to leave this home. It wasn't the house that was so special, but the people. She had found acceptance and compassion with Matthias and Fannie. She had found concern and thoughtfulness and a desire to help her, and it had warmed her heart.

Leaving this Amish home and these wonderful people would be hard, very, very hard.

Matthias scooted his chair back from the table and shook his head. "I fear Lily is making a mistake," he told his mother.

She nodded in agreement. "I am concerned for her safety in town. She does not realize how isolated this farm is and how difficult it would be for this Peterson man to think to look for her here."

"Perhaps I can convince her to stay with us when I see her later today."

"She's determined, Matthias."

"Which doesn't mean that she's making good decisions."

His mother stared at him. "Be careful, my son."

"The man is not searching for me, *Mamm*."

"This I know, but I am not as worried about the man coming after you as I am about your interest in this woman."

Matthias raised his brow. "Did I not see a motherly concern for her in your eyes as well?"

His mother nodded. "She struggles with

the decisions her mother made, and my heart reaches out to her. There is much she needs to process, as the *Englisch* say."

Matthias needed to process a few things, too, like the way he enjoyed being with Lily and how his heart had reacted when he held her in the woods this morning. He had been worried about her safety then, but he had also been confused by the feelings that had made him hold on to her for longer than he should have. He had tried to brush off his thoughts about her as they drove home, yet he kept thinking about how natural it had felt to wrap her in his arms.

She had shared so much about her past and had been forthright about the rumors that continued to circulate concerning Noelle's death and her mother's involvement. He admired Lily for wanting to clear her mother's name, but he knew the task would probably be more than she—or any non-law enforcement person— could achieve. Lily needed to talk to Sheriff Granger even if it meant opening old wounds. Perhaps she could encourage the sheriff to revisit the murder case as well as search for Peterson.

How ironic that the man with a rifle in his duffel bag had brought Lily back to Sunview. She had planned to return to town today, but Peterson had made that a certainty. Now that she was here, she seemed committed to stop the hateful rumors once and for all.

Lily returned to the kitchen with her purse and overnight bag in hand and placed them near the door.

Fannie glanced at the wall clock and *tsked*. "We are already late into the day. Before you leave, you must eat something, dear." She opened the icebox where the perishables were kept and removed a plate of cold cuts and cheese.

"I'll get the plates and silverware." Lily retrieved the items from the cabinet and quickly set the table.

She filled three glasses with water as Matthias helped his mother arrange cold cuts, cheese and sliced bread on the table.

"There is a jar of applesauce in the pantry and sweet pickles and beets," Fannie said and hurried to retrieve them.

"Your mother is doing too much, Matthias."

He nodded knowingly at Lily. "She shows her love through the food she prepares."

A sweet smile graced Lily's face. "What a lovely thought. My mother was more of a pre-packaged cook. Bologna sandwiches were the usual lunch fare."

"Yet she did her best, *yah*?"

Lily's face clouded for a moment. "I'm not sure, but it was the life we lived."

Matthias didn't need to be told that Lily's relationship with her mother was less than perfect.

Fannie breezed back into the kitchen. "I found the jars." She opened them and placed them on the table, along with the serving utensils.

"Sit," she commanded.

Once seated at the table, they bowed their heads. Matthias peered at Lily, noting the intense look on her face as if she were beseeching the Lord to answer her prayer. Perhaps to clear her mother's name and solve Noelle's murder.

Matthias closed his eyes for a moment. *Keep her safe, Lord*, he prayed. *And allow me to help her in any way you see fit.*

He glanced up just as Lily opened her eyes. There was no sparkle in them, no twinkle, or laughter lines around her mouth. He saw her concern and anxiousness. Again, he lifted up his request to the Lord. *Keep her safe.*

Conversation was sparse as they ate slowly and methodically, as if none of them wanted their time together to come to an end. When they could no longer dally over their empty plates, Fannie pushed back from the table and carried her dish to the sink.

Lily and Matthias did the same so that they all bunched up around the counter.

"Coffee?" Fannie asked.

Lily shook her head. "The afternoon is passing, and I must get to town, but first, let me help you with the dishes."

"Absolutely not." Fannie pointed to a tray of freshly baked sweets. "Perhaps I can pack a few cookies in a bag for you to have this evening before you go to bed."

"Fannie, you're so generous, but I'll find something to eat in town."

"As I mentioned earlier, I have a four-thirty appointment," Matthias said. "I'll meet you after I'm done, and we can have dinner together at the City Café."

She smiled. "That would be nice, Matthias."

"When can you check in at the B and B?"

"After four o'clock, so anytime you arrive would be perfect. We could talk to Sheriff Granger before dinner."

"We'll do that, but first, call the B and B and make sure Peterson isn't a registered guest."

His mother turned on the water in the sink and pointed through the hallway to the main room. "Make your phone call in the living room so the running water does not disturb your conversation."

Lily followed his mother's suggestion. She settled onto a chair near the woodstove, tapped her cell a number of times and held the phone to her ear. Matthias dried the dishes his mother washed all while keeping an eye on Lily. From her pleasant expression when she returned to the kitchen, he felt her call had been successful.

"Peterson is not at the B and B, Matthias. You don't have to worry."

He was happy to hear the news, but he would continue to worry as long as Peterson was on the loose.

"Thank you for your wonderful hospitality." Lily stretched out her hand.

He placed the dish towel on the counter and stared at her, wishing for half a second that she would have opened her arms and embraced him a bit more enthusiastically.

Accepting her handshake, he felt a warmth envelop him. Their hands remained clasped for a long moment, until Fannie placed the last dish in the strainer and turned to stare at them.

"You are leaving now?" she stated the obvious.

Lily pulled her hand out of his hold and turned to hug his mother. "Thank you so much, Fannie."

"Remember that the guest room is available if the B and B is not to your liking."

"I'll remember. Be sure to tell the children how much I enjoyed meeting them."

"I am certain they would say the same to

you," Matthias offered. He knew Sarah and Toby would be disappointed when they returned from school and realized their newfound friend was no longer staying with them.

Matthias handed Lily her purse and grabbed her suitcase. "I'll see you at about five o'clock. We can visit the sheriff together."

"Thank you, Matthias. I appreciate your support."

He walked her to the barn and felt a sense of emptiness as he watched her drive away. Duke, as if realizing his upset, rubbed against his leg. He bent to pat the faithful dog. "Lily is a *gut* woman, *yah*, Duke?"

The dog nuzzled closer. "*Yah*, we will both miss the pretty *Englischer*. The children and my mother will as well."

How could a woman—an *Englisch* woman at that—have such an impact on his entire family? What he'd told Duke was true. Everyone would miss Lily, but Matthias would miss her most of all.

FIVE

Lily had never felt so confused. She needed to leave the Overholt family so she wouldn't draw danger to their peaceful life, even though Matthias had assured her that Peterson would never suspect she had managed to get to their house the night of the shooting.

She believed Matthias, although she knew it would be better for everyone if she moved to the B and B. Lily had told Peterson about the motel on the highway, but it was in an isolated location. The parking lot had never been well lit, and it wasn't the place for a woman alone to find lodging. She would feel much more secure at the B and B. Still, she would miss the warmth of Matthias's home, the laughter of his children and Fannie's caring gaze. Thinking back over her life, she had never felt so welcome and so at home with any other family, including her own.

Lily understood the reason for her mother's actions, but she couldn't condone them all, such as her tumultuous relationship with the sheriff, even though Lily would always blame Granger for sweeping her mother off her feet, so to speak. Her mother being so needy wasn't his fault, but the fact that he'd played into her need was.

The letter from Betsy was in Lily's pocket. As soon as she was checked in to her room, she'd call her friend. Thankfully, Betsy had included her mobile number in with her note.

Driving into town was a *déjà vu* moment, but not in a good way. Lily was overcome with memories of those last days before Christmas break, when the gossips were wreaking havoc with her mother's reputation, and the kids at school were turning their backs on Lily. Clay Lambert had continued to say hello, at least when he wasn't with Kevin Granger, and Betsy had remained a loyal friend through it all.

Glancing at the clock on the dashboard, she decided to stop at the garage before checking in to her room. If she remembered correctly, the mechanic's shop wasn't far from the B and B.

She braked at the red light and breathed in the town that had changed very little in the last five years. She spied the flower shop and movie theater, the small grocery store and a few office buildings before she turned onto a side street that led to the garage. A guy about her age in grease-stained overalls stepped toward her car when she pulled onto his lot. He wiped his hands on a rag and then stuck it in his back pocket as she climbed from her car and extended her hand.

"Lily Hudson." They shook.

"Greg Roberts." He glanced at her front left bumper. "Looks like you ran into something."

Not wanting to tell him what had happened, she said she'd misjudged a parking space. "I'd like you to check under the hood as well as fix the bumper. That mountain road is steep and treacherous, and I want to ensure everything's working before I head south."

"Yes, ma'am." The guy nodded. "Shouldn't take me long to bang out the dent and check the engine." He grabbed a clipboard from within the garage and held it out to her along with a ballpoint pen. "Fill out your name and address and leave a phone number where I can reach you."

"I'm staying at the B and B."

"Not a problem." He pointed to a narrow side street. "Take that road and turn into the first side alley. You'll come out at the rear of the B and B."

"I knew it was close by."

He nodded. "Yes, ma'am."

She filled out the form. "You'll call me when my car's ready?"

"I'll look it over and call you tonight if anything needs work, otherwise your car should be ready in the morning."

"How early do you open?"

"Seven a.m."

"Sounds good." Lily grabbed her overnight bag, purse and laptop from the car, handed him the key and glanced around the surrounding area. Not that she thought Peterson would be hovering close by, but she needed to be careful. Her shoulder was still sore, and she had a bruise on her hip thanks to her run-in with him last night. She didn't want any more scrapes or bruises.

A horse and buggy turned onto the side road. The Amish driver nodded as he passed by, and the *clip-clop* of the mare's hooves took her back to Matthias's farm. She thought again of the sturdy furniture he made and the feel of the table where the family gathered. Matthias was a talented man. Perhaps he didn't realize how many people would pay top dollar for the furniture he created. When he joined her this evening, she would be sure to compliment him on his woodworking.

Lily pulled in a deep breath when she turned into the narrow alleyway. Peterson could be anywhere. Perhaps coming to town had been a mistake, after all. A noise like rustling paper sounded to her right. A stray dog loped toward her. She could tell he was old from the gray in his coat, and his wagging tail showed his friendliness. She rubbed his back and smiled, thinking of Duke and wishing he were with her now.

"Aren't you a nice dog?" she said.

The sound of footsteps made her turn toward the street. A man hurried past the entrance to the alley. The guy was tall and full-figured, but in a muscular way. He wore a dark-knit cap pulled over his head and a camouflage jacket.

Her pulse raced, and her heart pounded in her chest. Seeing only the man's back, she couldn't be sure who it was, but the camo jacket made her more than nervous. She left the dog and hurried to the rear entrance of the B and B. Once she entered the old Victorian home, she breathed a sigh of relief.

Glancing back through the window, she saw no one. Maybe her imagination was getting the better of her.

The young male receptionist at the desk wore a name tag that read Quin. He wasn't the person Lily had talked to on the phone, but he was cordial and welcoming. Again, Lily inquired about seeing anyone who limped and had a beard and a camo jacket.

Quin shrugged. "You see anything and everything in Sunview this time of year."

"Is anyone matching that description staying here?"

"Not that I know of," he said. "But I've haven't been on duty long."

After she had signed the necessary forms, the clerk stepped into a small rear office. Large old-fashioned brass keys hung on a pegboard near a picture window. Quin wrote Lily's last name on a paper tag he attached to a hook under the room number and handed her the key. "Let me know if you leave. I'll hang the key on the peg board and give it back to you when you return."

"I haven't seen that type of a key system in a long time."

He smiled. "It goes with the Victorian ambiance. Folks like the historic charm."

Lily glanced around the lovely furnishings and attractive art that decorated the room. "The owner has lovely taste."

"You can tell her in the morning. Breakfast is served between seven and nine thirty. If you need an earlier to-go box, that can be arranged as well."

"The owner thinks of everything."

"Yes, ma'am." Quin pointed to a side hallway. "Your room is the second on the left. You have a view of the side patio and garden and a portion of the main street, as well."

"By the way—" Lily turned back to the clerk

"—I'm expecting a visitor to stop by later this afternoon. Will you call my room when he arrives?"

Quin pointed to a rotary phone on a side table. "I'll give him the number, and he can make the call."

Lily glanced at the front door. "What's your policy about the doors?"

"Policy?" He raised his brow, then as if he finally comprehended what she was asking, he nodded. "One can never be too careful. The rear and side doors are locked at all times, although you can exit through both of them. The front door is locked at nine each evening. Ring the doorbell, if you come in after that time. Someone is always on duty."

Satisfied that she would remain safe through the night, Lily headed to her room. A slight musty smell greeted her, which was often the case in older accommodations. The bed was covered with a white duvet and a number of pillows in matching white cases were propped against the back of the bed. A small television sat on a desk and an overstuffed chair took up the corner near the dresser.

A cool breeze came in through the window. She pushed back the draperies to find it open. Probably to draw fresh air into the stuffy room. Lily closed the window and tried to engage the lock, but it seemed to have been painted over far too many times.

She picked up the phone and tapped zero for the front desk. The clerk answered. "How may I help you?"

"I just checked into 102. The room is lovely, but I can't get the window to lock."

"Yes, ma'am. You don't have to worry here in Sunview. People leave their doors unlocked, as well as their windows."

That wasn't what Lily wanted to hear. "Could I switch rooms?"

"I'm sorry, ma'am, but the other rooms are occupied. I could ask our maintenance man to see if he can fix the lock."

"That would be fine. When should I expect him?"

"Tomorrow morning after eight. He left here about thirty minutes ago."

Lily sighed as she hung up and glanced again at the window. Peering outside, she saw the sidewalk that meandered through the garden and led to the street in front and the alleyway in the rear.

So much for a good night's sleep.

She pulled Betsy's letter from her pocket, along with her cell, and tapped in the number her friend had provided. The call went to voice mail. "Leave a message and I'll get back to you."

Eying the clock again, she wondered if she should head to the sheriff's office but then thought better of it. Facing Doug Granger would be difficult enough with Matthias's support. She didn't feel up to going there on her own.

She scooted the desk chair next to the window and angled the seat so she could watch the occasional cars and buggies pass by on the main street.

The ebb and flow of traffic, scant though it was, calmed her anxiety. Sunview was a sleepy little tourist town, especially in the colder months. People considered it a family-friendly destination. She would be fine here.

The late afternoon sun came through the window and lulled her into a drowsy mood. She folded her arms on the windowsill and rested her head on her arms. Before long, she had drifted into a light slumber.

The shrill ring of a telephone pulled her awake. She rubbed her eyes, trying to get her bearings, and then hurried to answer the phone, expecting to hear Matthias's voice.

"This is Greg at the garage."

She glanced at her cell on the desk. "I... I thought you'd call my cell."

"It went to voice mail. You said you were staying at the B and B. I've got bad news, ma'am."

She almost groaned aloud. "How expensive is the repair going to be?"

"I won't charge you. I should have locked your car, but we don't worry much in these parts."

She glanced at the window. "So what's the problem? Is it something with the engine?"

"Actually it's the rear floor mats. The stuff in the trunk's been messed with pretty badly, too, but nothing appears to have been taken."

Lily pushed the phone closer to her ear. "I don't understand."

"Someone broke into your car. Except it wasn't locked, so I should say someone riffled through your car. The rear floor mats have some gashes in them. Looks like it was done with a box cutter. All that craft stuff in your trunk's been rummaged through as well, as if the person was searching for something." He sighed. "I'll order new mats and install them without charge. Can't tell you how upset I am about this. I called the sheriff's department. Someone's on their way. How soon can you get here?"

She raked her hand through her hair, still groggy and trying to make sense of what had happened.

"Give me a few minutes."

Lily hung up and shoved her case and laptop into the closet, grateful she had thought to bring her computer to the lodge. In the lobby, she stopped to give her key to the clerk and tell him where she would be. "If a gentleman stops by, please let him know I'm at the garage."

"Greg's place?"

"That's right."

"Will do. Have a good night."

Lily's night was already ruined. Who would damage her floor mats and rummage through her car? She rubbed her hands over her arms and shivered. She knew who would do exactly that.

Pete Peterson.

Matthias's meeting took longer than he had expected, and he arrived at the B and B closer to five thirty. He tied his mare to a hitching post and hurried inside to ask the clerk to let Lily know he was in the lobby.

"Sir, she left here not long ago."

"Do you know where she went?"

"To Sunview Garage on the next street over." He pointed through the back door. "You can cut through the alleyway."

Matthias left his mare and buggy at the B and B and hurried around the corner. His heart stopped when he saw one of the sheriff department's sedans parked in front of the garage with lights flashing.

He spotted Lily talking to a deputy and let

out a sigh of relief. He glanced at her car. The trunk was open, and the crafts that had been neatly arranged appeared to have been tossed about helter-skelter.

Lily glanced up as he approached.

"Are you all right?" he asked.

She nodded. "This is Deputy Walker. He's on duty tonight. The sheriff's out of town and not expected back until tomorrow morning."

Matthias nodded to the deputy and then turned back to Lily. "What happened?"

"Someone rummaged through the trunk of my car. It looks like nothing was taken, but the floor mats in the rear were cut with what appears to have been a box cutter or some type of X-Acto knife." Lily stared at him, her eyes wide. "I told the deputy about Peterson. It's got to be him."

"How did he know you were in town?"

"I'm not sure. Maybe he saw my car when he was passing by. Earlier, I saw someone wearing a camo jacket. I didn't see his face, but it could have been Pete."

"We'll put out a Be On the Lookout for him," the deputy said. "I'm not sure why he cut the back floor mats. If any ideas come to mind, let me know."

The flash drive, Matthias thought, but he remained silent.

The deputy handed Lily a form and a business card. "Here's a copy of the statement you filled out earlier, ma'am, as well as my card. Call me if you have any more problems. As I mentioned, the sheriff will be back tomorrow if you want to talk to him."

"Thank you, Deputy Walker. You'll contact me if you spot anyone who looks like Peterson?"

"Will do. Camo's pretty popular around here, but with the limp and beard—" He paused. "You never know about these guys. They like to stir up trouble, that's for sure. Watch yourself, ma'am," he said before heading to his squad car.

Greg stepped forward. "Look, I'm really sorry. I'll work on getting those floor mats. A truck comes up the mountain tomorrow. I'll place the order tonight and insist the mats are on that truck and call you when your car's ready."

"What about tonight?" Matthias asked. "Can you park her car in the bay and lock the garage so no more damage is done?"

"That's exactly what I'll do."

Matthias took Lily's arm and ushered her along the sidewalk. "You need to come back to my farm, Lily. If Pete saw your car, he'll know you're staying in Sunview and probably someplace close to the garage." He urged her along. "That means the B and B."

"I told you before that I don't want to bring danger to your family."

"And I told you that Peterson will never suspect you made it all the way to my farm. He'll be searching along Mountain Road and now in town. You'll be safe with me."

"I'm staying in town just for tonight. Once my car is ready, I'll head home to my cabin."

Matthias was frustrated by her stubbornness and groaned under his breath.

They approached the B and B from the street, and Lily pointed suddenly to one of the windows.

"Matthias, look," she whispered. "Someone's trying to get into Room 102. That's my room."

A man wearing latex gloves had pulled one of the wrought iron patio chairs under her window. The sun was setting, and it was hard to make out the man's face, but it was easy enough to spot his knit cap and camo jacket.

"Stop," Lily called.

Matthias pulled her protectively behind a row of bushes so neither of them would be seen.

The guy glanced ever so briefly toward the street as if searching for the person who had sounded the alarm before he jumped down and raced away through the rear alley.

"Come on," Matthias encouraged her. "We need to get you inside and call the deputy."

But Lily had pulled out her cell phone and had already connected with the deputy.

"He tried to break into my room at the B and B," she said into her phone. "Peterson's in the area. You've got to apprehend him. Now!"

Sirens sounded in the downtown area just as Deputy Walker rushed into the garden of the B and B. "You called me before I left the area. I've sent two squad cars to search for your assailant. We'll find him."

Lily wasn't so sure.

Deputy Walker took down more information as the hotel clerk hovered nearby, worried about the flashing lights on the squad car and the upset it would cause the other guests.

"How did he know which room was yours?" the deputy asked.

Lily motioned him to follow her to the large window in the office situated behind the registration desk. Matthias joined them there. She pointed through the window to the pegboard where a tag bearing her name hung under her room number. "See what's hanging from the peg that reads Room 102?"

The deputy nodded. "Your last name."

"That's right. All Peterson had to do was look at the board to determine which room I was staying in. When he peered through the various windows, he could probably read the room number written on the inside of each bedroom door. Mine is the second room along the downstairs hallway, 102. Fairly easy to determine which one was mine."

"That made it too easy for him," the deputy said. "I'll talk to the owner of the B and B. She needs a new safer key system."

The deputy searched the patio and checked for prints on the windowsill and wrought iron chair. When Walker finished his investigation and climbed into his patrol car, Matthias took her arm.

"You're leaving Sunview tonight and returning home with me," he insisted.

Tired as she was and with her nerves frayed, she was happy to go with Matthias. The clerk seemed glad she was leaving. "No charge for the room," he told her.

"I had reservations for additional nights."

"Shall I cancel them?" he asked.

"Definitely," Matthias insisted.

Lily gathered her laptop and travel bag from her room. Matthias carried them to his buggy and placed them in the back, then helped Lily into the second seat. "Sit back here in case we pass Peterson on the road leaving town. I want him to think you're still in Sunview."

Matthias didn't have to tell her to be careful.

Peterson had found her once. She had to ensure he didn't find her again.

Her stomach soured. Too much was happening too fast, and she couldn't put the pieces together.

At least she had a place to stay tonight. She was grateful for Matthias and his mother. Tomorrow, she would be able to think more clearly and find a way to clear her mother's name and bring Peterson to justice before she headed south to her cabin. Two huge tasks that she wasn't up to dwelling on tonight. Her head would be able to make better sense of things in the morning, and she could come up with a plan. Right now, all she could think about was Matthias driving her home and making sure she was safe. She would never forget what the handsome Amish man had done for her. Nor would she ever forget how he had come to her rescue.

SIX

When Lily didn't show up for breakfast the next morning, Matthias tried to reassure the twins that she was resting and would hopefully see them after school. At least, he wanted her to still be with them and not on the Mountain Road heading back to her cabin.

After taking the children to school in the buggy, he returned home and was relieved to find Lily helping his mother in the kitchen. She seemed subdued, and fatigue lined her pretty face.

"I'm sorry I didn't get up early enough to see Sarah and Toby," she said as she poured Matthias a cup of coffee. "I didn't sleep well and finally dozed off sometime after five."

He nodded his thanks as he took the cup she offered. "You've been through so much and needed the sleep."

"Still." She shrugged. "It's not like me. I tried to call my friend Betsy this morning. For some reason, her phone keeps going to voice mail, but it won't let me leave a message."

Fannie chortled from the sink where she was washing the morning dishes. "This technology is something we do not have to worry about."

"At times, that might be a blessing." Lily glanced at Matthias. "I'll call the garage in an hour or so to see if Greg got the floor mats. Would you mind taking me to town when my car's ready?"

"You're still planning on leaving Sunview?"

"After I talk to the sheriff."

"And what about Betsy?" he asked.

She sighed. "I'm not sure what I'll do if I can't reach her."

"You could stay another day," Fannie suggested.

Yesterday, Lily had been determined to clear her mother's name and bring Noelle's killer to justice. Today, she seemed to have accepted the reality that both tasks might be impossible for her to achieve.

"Once you hear from the garage, we can use your cell phone to call the Amish taxi," Matthias said.

Her brow raised. "What about your buggy?"

"If we take a taxi, you'll have to drive me back to the farm after we get your car and see the sheriff."

Matthias's heart warmed when she smiled and shook her head ever so slightly.

"You're trying to keep me here for another day," she said.

"*Yah*. That's exactly what I'm trying to do. Plus, the children would love to see you again."

"Then it is settled," Fannie added.

"Both of you are ganging up on me." Lily laughed under her breath. "One more night."

"*Gut.*"

Just as they had discussed earlier, Matthias used Lily's cell to the call the Amish taxi after Greg at the garage notified her that her car was ready to be picked up.

"Both of you, be careful," Fannie cautioned when the taxi pulled into the drive.

Duke met them outside and nuzzled Lily's leg. She patted the dog's back. "Such a good boy."

"Stay here," Matthias said. "And take care of *Mamm* while we're gone."

The dog stopped at the bottom of the porch steps, his tail wagging.

"Duke's a good watch dog," she said as Matthias opened the taxi's rear door and held it open for Lily.

"He's a great dog, but he's a bit spoiled, as my mother likes to point out." Matthias chuckled and slipped into the back seat next to her.

He had told the driver their destination over

the phone, but he repeated it for clarity and then focused his gaze on the road ahead as well as the intersecting farm roads.

"You're worried Pete might spot us," Lily said, no doubt seeing his concern.

"I'm hoping he's left Sunview and is headed farther north. You said he mentioned Mountain Crest that first night. The best possible situation would be if he's holed up there and never returns this way again."

Lily nodded. "That's my hope as well."

Once they entered town, Lily pointed to the small restaurant next to the drugstore. "I got my first job washing dishes at the City Café when I turned sixteen."

"It's the best eatery in town." He smiled. "Of course, we don't have many restaurants to choose from."

"The kids used to go there Friday nights for ice-cream sundaes and banana splits."

"Sarah and Toby love those." He wondered if Lily ever joined in the fun or if she always had to work.

Pointing to the next block, he added, "The candy store on the corner is new. My mother enjoys their pralines and admits they're better than she can make."

"After we pick up my car, let's stop there before we see the sheriff. I'd like to get Fannie something to show my appreciation for taking care of me that first night and for her hospitability."

"That's thoughtful of you, Lily, although not necessary."

"It's something I want to do."

The taxi dropped them at the garage. Greg stood by her car as if he had been waiting for her.

"New mats." He opened the rear door so she could see the upgrade he had provided. "I tried to tidy your items in the trunk and ran it through the car wash. Again, I'm so sorry about what happened." He handed her the keys, and Lily thanked him for all he had done.

Matthias flicked his gaze over the side streets and the entrance to the alley that led to the B and B, making sure Peterson was nowhere in sight. Seeing no sign of a man in camo, he slipped into the front seat next to Lily. "Remember that you need to be careful while you're in town."

She nodded. "You're right, but I can't halt my life because of a guy who thinks he can push his weight around."

"He's got a pistol and a rifle, Lily, which means he has the upper hand."

"I know. He's well-armed, but I won't let him take control of my life."

Matthias recalled what his mother had said

about Lily being determined. A good attribute, yet it could cause her problems. She needed to be smarter and faster than the guy with the weapons. Matthias needed to be as well in order to keep her safe.

"We'll worry about Peterson later." She pulled into a parking space in front of the candy shop. "Right now, I've got some shopping to do. What would the children enjoy? Lollipops were always a favorite of mine."

"Don't all children love lollipops?"

"Exactly."

Lily bought a box of pralines for Fannie and an assortment of lollipops for the children. She smiled at Matthias. "What can I get you?"

He held up his hand. "Nothing, but let's have lunch at the café after we talk to the sheriff."

"You're not worried about Peterson?"

"We can watch the street through the window."

"Okay, but lunch is my treat."

Matthias shook his head. "Amish men always pick up the check when they dine with a lady friend."

"Am I a lady friend?" she teased.

The strain he had read earlier in her gaze eased, and a warmth spread across his chest. "You're a lady, and we're friends."

"Exactly."

"I'll put the candy in the car," he suggested. "Then we can walk to the sheriff's office. It's on the next block."

As he opened the back door of Lily's car, he heard her gasp. He placed the purchases on the seat, slammed the door and glanced at where he had left her.

She was gone. "Lily?"

His heart pounded a warning just as he saw her running along the side street. He raced after her. She was about fifty yards ahead of him when she stopped abruptly, made an about-face and ran back.

"Are you all right?" he asked as she neared.

She glanced over her shoulder. "A man came out of the drugstore dressed in a camo jacket. He had long hair and a scruffy beard." She paused to catch her breath. "I hurried to the corner, hoping to get a clearer view, and my heart nearly stopped when he crossed the street. Seeing him in profile—"

He rubbed his hand over her shoulder.

"It was Peterson. I didn't want to lose sight of him, so I followed, taking care that he didn't see me. At the next corner, he glanced back. His eyes widened, and he started running toward me."

"He's gone now." Matthias glanced at the empty corner where Lily claimed Peterson had seen her before he ushered her back to her car. "Let's drive to the sheriff's office. He needs to know what's happening."

Matthias was worried about Lily's safety as well as her irrational behavior. Peterson was dangerous, yet she had followed him. If she weren't so upset now, he would talk to her about being more careful and not putting herself in dangerous positions.

Yes, Lily was determined, too determined, and that was the problem. Matthias needed to make certain she acted rationally and didn't get hurt again. Pete Peterson was a real threat, and for whatever reason, he kept coming after Lily.

Lily was trembling when she entered the sheriff's office, partially because of her run-in with Peterson, and partially because she didn't want to face Granger. She hadn't liked him when he was involved with her mother, and she'd liked him less after that relationship had ended. For too many nights, she had listened to her mother cry herself to sleep. Lily had decided then and there to protect her own heart. She didn't need a man in her life. Period.

"We're here to see Sheriff Granger," Matthias told the deputy behind the counter.

Sawyer was written on his name tag. He appeared to be pushing forty and was a bit overweight, but his expression was pleasant. The deputy called the sheriff and evidently got approval for their visit. He grabbed a file folder off the counter and walked them to an office at the end of a long hallway.

After tapping twice, he opened the door. "Sir, these are the folks who wanted to see you."

The man behind the desk stood. He was still tall and muscular, but his hair was gray and dark circles hung under his eyes. He looked much older than Lily remembered, although five years had passed since she'd last seen him.

"Thank you, Deputy Sawyer." She stepped into the sheriff's office and watched a wave of confusion pass over his face.

"Lily?"

She introduced Matthias and they both settled into the chairs in front of the sheriff's desk.

"I read Deputy Walker's report about what happened last night. How can I help you today?" he asked as he got over his surprise at seeing her and returned to his seat.

She explained about driving the man in camo to Sunview and what had happened since then. "He hesitated before telling me his name was Pete Peterson, so I'm not sure if that's his real name."

Granger nodded and made a couple of notes

on a paper he pulled from the folder his deputy had given him. "Any idea why he's in the area?"

She glanced at Matthias and then back at the sheriff. "Only that he wanted to go to Mountain Crest. It was late, and I agreed to take him as far as the motel on the highway."

"Sounds like you never got there."

She nodded. "If Matthias hadn't found me, I'm not sure what would have happened."

The sheriff made another notation before he eyed Matthias. "Evidently, something alerted you that there could be a problem?"

"I heard gunshots. Lily's shoulder was grazed."

To his credit, the sheriff appeared concerned. "Did you go to the clinic? There's a doc on duty 24/7."

"Matthias's mother dressed the wound. It's healing."

She provided a description of Peterson and explained about finding him on Mountain Road after his car had run into the ditch. "A radio announcement said a white sedan had been stolen and the driver was dangerous."

Granger pursed his lips. "I'll check that out. Any identifying marks on Mr. Peterson?"

"He limps. He said his leg was injured in the past, and he mentioned being in the army."

Even though the sheriff had read Deputy Walker's report from last night, she explained about her car being ransacked and about the man who had tried to open the window of her room at the B and B.

Granger nodded. "As I mentioned, I saw Walker's report. We sent out a BOLO, and our department is actively searching for him."

Lily sighed with relief. At least Granger seemed concerned and was being proactive.

He pursed his lips and studied the notes he had made before he glanced at her again. "Is there anything else you can tell me?"

She thought of the flash drive. Maybe it was sour grapes after what had happened in the past, but Lily didn't want to hand the device or the files over to the sheriff. Yet, he needed to have all the facts in order to handle the investigation.

Thankful that she had copied the files on the flash drive to her computer and her phone, she opened her purse, pulled out the small device and placed it on Granger's desk.

"I believe Peterson mistakenly left this on the floor of my car." She explained about the three files. "I have a feeling he's interested in the Christmas Lodge."

The sheriff raised his brow. "Because of the brochure?"

"There's that. Plus, he became agitated when I mentioned that he could stay there."

"Let's hope your feeling doesn't pan out. As

you probably know, the festival is in a couple days, and the last thing we need is trouble at the lodge."

"I fear you'll have worse problems if you don't find him. He's dangerous, and he's packing a pistol and a rifle."

"Be assured, Lily, that my deputies and I will do everything in our power to track down Mr. Peterson, or whatever his name may be. I presume you have a cell phone so I can contact you if anything develops?"

She gave him her cell number. Granger wrote it on a separate piece of notepaper and stapled it to the file folder on his desk.

"I'll let you know if we find him, but the information you provided could fit a lot of men in this area. If you think of anything else, let me know. The city is filling up. People are coming to town for the festival and to shop. We've got lots of newcomers in the area. Most of them are good folks, although some of them are here to cause a little trouble." He splayed his hands. "As you can imagine, we've got a lot on our plate."

"I'm sure you do." Lily heard the sarcasm in her tone.

"Now, Lily—"

"I'm not a teenager, Sheriff."

He smiled. "That's evident."

"And I don't appreciate your condescension." She rose. Matthias did as well.

"I'll be in touch," Granger said as they headed for the door.

Before she stepped out of his office, he called to her. "I failed to ask about your mother. How's Violet?"

Lily wouldn't tell him the truth about her mother's declining health and inability to remember what she had done ten minutes earlier. The doctors claimed it was age, but Lily knew her mother's heartbreak added to the mix. A woman who had been down and out most of her life had given her heart to a man who'd promised her everything, but it had all been a lie. She was a woman who'd gone from being poor to destitute and unable to take care of her only child—

No, Lily wouldn't tell him the truth.

"My mother's fine, Granger. Just fine. Nice of you to ask." Then she left his office and slammed the door behind her.

Matthias's eyes widened ever so slightly, but to his credit, he didn't appear nonplussed in any way. Instead, he kept his head high as he walked at her side.

Seeing Granger again in her lifetime would be too soon, yet Lily knew that in order to bring Pete Peterson to justice, she would have to work with the sheriff even though she didn't want to. Finding a dangerous man was more important than her own feelings or any memories she wanted to keep buried in the past.

Matthias took her arm. "I don't know about you, but I'm no longer hungry. Heading back to the farm is probably a better idea than eating at the City Café."

She nodded. "I agree."

Together they hurried to her car. She slid behind the wheel as Matthias continued to study the street as if searching for anyone who looked threatening.

She breathed a sigh of relief once they turned onto the roadway that led to his farm. She had faced Sheriff Granger and survived. Now she had to decide whether to go home tomorrow or remain in Sunview. She didn't know what to do, especially with Matthias sitting next to her. He made her lightheaded and confused, which wasn't like her at all. She needed to think rationally before she decided about tomorrow.

Right now, all she could think of was getting through the evening with the handsome farmer and his adorable children. Toby and Sarah had stolen her heart as soon as they entered the kitchen yesterday morning. Once again, she glanced at Matthias. Yes, she was drawn to his children, but she was also drawn to him.

SEVEN

Matthias spent most of the afternoon catching up on farm work. Later in the day, his mother left the house and headed to the buggy.

"I'm picking up the children from school. Lily is tending the stew that's simmering on the stove. She's also making dinner rolls." His mother's brow raised. "Her own recipe. That is not what I expected."

"You always underestimate the *Englisch*," he said with a smile.

"*Yah*, and there is reason. Most are lazy and self-absorbed."

"You see through a different gaze, *Mamm*. Perhaps Lily will change your mind."

"She is an anomaly, this is for certain."

When the children returned home, their smiling faces when they climbed down from the buggy assured him that they were eager to see their houseguest.

"Miss Lily is still here?" Sarah asked as she hugged him and planted a soft kiss on his cheek.

"She is in the house, probably waiting to play jacks with you."

"And pick-up sticks," Toby added as he, too, hugged Matthias.

"Get a snack, then homework, then finish your chores. You'll have time to play after the evening meal."

They both nodded and ran together into the house. He heard Lily's exuberant greeting, and the laughter that flowed through the open doorway warmed his heart. His children hadn't seemed so lighthearted in years.

He rubbed his jaw and shook his head. No doubt, living with a widower father had dampened some of their enthusiasm. A woman brought heart to a home. His mother was getting up in age and didn't have the energy to play with the children. By the end of the day, she was tired and feeling her arthritis.

For so long, Matthias had been focused on overcoming his grief—and guilt—that he hadn't paid as much attention as he should have to his children.

He glanced upward and shook his head. "Forgive me, *Gott*, for putting my needs first."

Perhaps Lily had come into their lives to shake him out of his self-absorption. She might be a wake-up call, of sorts, to encourage him to spend more quality time with the children. He needed to bring laughter back to their house and to their sweet faces. Life was not all work and not all mourning the loss of a loved one. His mother had told him that on more than one occasion.

He should tell Lily how she had helped him move beyond the past, at least in part. Lily had mentioned earlier that she was grateful for their hospitality. She needed to know that he was grateful for her help as well.

After completing the day's chores, he washed at the pump, dried his hands and arms on the towel hanging nearby and hurried into the house. The rich scent of a stew, thick with tomatoes and onions and garlic, as well as the mouthwatering aroma of rolls in the oven welcomed him along with the smiling faces of his children. Lily sat between Sarah and Toby at the kitchen table, reviewing the children's homework papers.

She glanced up slowly. Her blue eyes, upturned mouth and rosy cheeks caused a rush of heat to warm his flesh. They locked eyes for a long moment while he tried to recall the last time he had been so overcome with attraction.

"We are almost finished with our work," Sarah declared, interrupting the emotion-packed moment he and Lily had shared.

The pink in Lily's cheeks darkened. She seemed as flustered as he was when she held up a paper. "Sarah has done her math and has gotten every problem right."

"*Gut*, Sarah." Matthias smiled at his daughter.

"And—" Lily reached for the writing tablet in front of his son "—Toby has done equally well. Plus, both children know their spelling words for this week as well as their science lesson."

His mother hurried into the kitchen to stir the stew. "Children, help your father with the chores."

Matthias held up his hand. "The work is done for this evening."

His mother pursed her lips.

"Do they have time to play a few games with Miss Lily?" he asked.

An unexpected smile graced his mother's lips, and she pointed toward the hallway. "Put away your papers, children, then take Lily into the main room. There is space near the stove for jacks and pick-up sticks."

The children scrambled to return their homework to their book bags, then Sarah took Lily's hand and nearly pulled her into the other room.

At the doorway, Lily glanced back. "Join us, Matthias." She glanced at his mother. "Unless Fannie needs your help."

His mother made a shooing motion. "Go,

Matthias. Be with your children. The stew must cook a bit longer. I can manage here."

Lily called out to Fannie from the main room. "The rolls will be ready to take from the oven in about ten minutes."

"Do not worry. I'll keep them warm in a covered bread basket."

Matthias smiled at his mother before he headed into the larger room. From all appearances, Lily had softened his mother's heart. Thinking back, he couldn't recall her ever bending the rules of their daily routine. But now that Lily was with them, the children's happiness was more important than chores.

Matthias sat on the floor next to Lily as the children pulled their games from the bookcase.

"First jacks, then pick-up sticks," Sarah announced.

"Fifteen minutes for each game," Toby added.

As Sarah threw the jacks on the floor and bounced the small rubber ball, Lily's laughter once again filled the house. The warm fire, the happy smiles of his children and the closeness of a beautiful woman who had awakened a forgotten need filled Matthias with a sense of satisfaction he hadn't felt since Rachel died.

A car screeched on the road outside the house. Duke barked a warning. Lily bristled and sent him a nervous glance. He rose from the floor and headed to the front door.

Stepping onto the porch, he spied the taillights of a car racing along the roadway, heading back to town. Probably a kid on *rumspringa*, but Matthias needed to keep up his guard. He stared after the car and watched as it disappeared into the distance. Once again, his attention had been focused on Lily instead of the reality of her situation.

He peered back into the house where she sat with the children. "Stay inside. I want to check the barn and outbuildings."

His mother stepped into the main room. "Take care, Matthias," she cautioned.

"Lock the doors until I return."

He left the house and noticed the streak of rubber that had been left on the roadway. He doubted Peterson would know where Lily was staying, yet Matthias needed to be vigilant to protect not only his family, but also Lily. Life was fragile. He knew that all too well. He could not and would not let another woman die because of his lack of action.

The Amish were peacekeepers, but he could not let trouble come to his family, even if the bishop would question his rationale. His family came first, no matter what the Amish believed.

"*Gott*, help me do the right thing," he said

as he stared at the surrounding hillside. "Help me to keep my family safe. Help me keep Lily safe as well."

The frivolity of the night had been dampened by the screech of tires on pavement. Lily had tried to keep from revealing her upset to the children, but they seemed to sense that the peaceful evening had been threatened.

Once Matthias came back inside, Fannie called them to the table. When they lowered their heads in prayer, Lily silently asked protection for the Overholt family and forgiveness for bringing danger to their doorstep. She hoped the racing car was driven by a teenager eager to push his newfound freedom to the limits and not the man who seemed intent to do her harm.

Glancing up, she realized everyone was staring at her. "Sorry." Evidently, she had taken too long with the blessing.

Matthias's brow raised, and she read the question in his gaze. She shrugged ever so lightly as if to share her own confusion about what had happened.

With the click of the silverware on the plates and the nourishment of the thick stew, the children's good humor returned, and they talked about some of the things that had happened at school.

"Our teacher found a frog in the cloak area," Toby shared. "She insisted one of the boys had brought it in his book bag. Levi Keim said he had seen the frog when he hung up his coat, and he was the first one there in the morning."

"Rebecca Troyer admitted she had a pet frog that often followed her to school," Sarah added. "Then our teacher said all pets must remain outside."

"Davey Zook has a pet snake, and the teacher said it couldn't come to school." Toby's eyes were wide as he added, "Not long after that, Davey asked to go outside. Mary Anne looked out the window and saw him take the snake out of his lunch box and lay it on the ground."

"Such a busy day," Lily interjected. "How could you focus on your work with so many surprises at school?"

"It was difficult," Toby admitted, looking older than his years.

Matthias reached for the bread basket. "Has anyone tried Lily's rolls?"

Both children nodded. "They are so *gut*."

"You need to thank Lily for making them."

"Thank you, Miss Lily," the children said in unison.

"You are most welcome, and thank you for letting me stay with you."

Lily enjoyed the children's stories and found

herself smiling at the menagerie of creatures that the teacher had had to put up with in her classroom. She ate slowly to appreciate the layers of flavor in the stew, but also to enjoy the time with the precious children.

Once everyone had eaten, Lily started to clear the table. "Fannie, you sit by the fire and let me do the dishes tonight."

"That would make me feel useless." Fannie pointed to the living area. "You have time for more games."

"But, *Mammi*, what about dessert?" Sarah asked.

"After your games. Now, hurry to play before I change my mind."

"Come with us, Miss Lily." The children pulled Lily from the table.

"Let's clear the table and rinse the dishes before we leave your *mammi* with all the work," she suggested, hoping to redirect the children.

Toby nodded. "If we work together, we can get it done quickly."

Lily made a game of clearing the table. She ran water into the dishpan and quickly scrubbed the soup bowls and bread plates. Before Fannie could get the coffeepot ready to brew, the washed dishes were in the strainer and the table was wiped clean. Matthias grabbed a broom and swept the floor while his mother watched the whirlwind of activity with a satisfied smile on her round face.

"Thank you for helping," she said. "I'll call you when the coffee is ready."

The children took turns with the games, and once again, laughter filled the house. Lily noticed Matthias turning his gaze to the window whenever a sound came from outside, but he didn't allow the children to see his concern.

After the jacks and pick-up sticks were put away, they gathered once again at the table for cookies and milk while the adults sipped coffee. Lily couldn't remember when last she had enjoyed herself so much, and in spite of Pete Peterson still being on the loose, she felt at peace in the warmth of the Amish home.

The children gave her a hug before they said good-night and climbed the stairs for bed. Matthias followed after them to tuck them in while Lily cleared the table once again.

"It has been a long day," Fannie admitted. "Matthias may want another cup of coffee when he comes downstairs, but I am going to my room, if you do not mind."

"Of course, Fannie. Thank you for a delicious dinner."

"And thanks to you for the rolls. Tell Matthias good night for me and have a restful sleep yourself."

Matthias joined Lily in the kitchen soon after Fannie had gone upstairs. "Your mother said to tell you good night."

"I think the excitement of having a guest in the house has tired her out."

"Then I need to leave tomorrow. I don't want to cause any problems."

"She won't hear of it, and neither will I. Besides, we need to go to the Christmas Lodge in the morning. You'll come, too. We set up the booths each year for the Christmas festival. A number of Amish families sell various handcrafted items. *Mamm* has been working for months on afghans and aprons. She's completed a few lap quilts and will also sell baked goods."

"You saw the items in my car from the last craft fair," Lily said. "I'd love to donate my things to your table. It's the least I can do after all you've done for me."

"No donations," he insisted. "You can sell them at our booth and earn the money for yourself."

"I have handmade ornaments and grapevine wreaths that always do well at this time of year. I'll leave them with you."

"Absolutely not. You need to go with us tomorrow."

She sighed, wanting to take him up on his offer, but she was confused as to what to do.

"When you go to the Christmas Lodge, I'll stop by the sheriff's office and make my decision depending upon whether Peterson has been apprehended."

"I didn't think you wanted to see Sheriff Granger again."

"I don't, but I want to remind him that Pete Peterson is still on the loose. What I know of the sheriff from the past is that he lets important things slide. I need to remind him that for the safely of his town, he needs to find Peterson."

"I don't want to pry, Lily, but what happened after you and your mother left Sunview?"

She glanced at the aluminum pot warming on the stove. "Your mother said you might want a second cup of coffee."

He nodded. "If we can sit together and discuss the past."

She refilled both their cups and joined him at the table. They both took a sip of the hot brew.

Lily lowered her cup and sighed. "It's a tangled story, but I can give you a quick overview."

"Whatever you decide works for me."

"As you know, when my mother realized the truth about Sheriff Granger, she was heartbroken. It was a few days before the Christmas break of my senior year. I wanted to graduate in the spring with my class even though I was always the outsider and never had a group of friends to pal around with like the other kids."

"So you didn't want to leave."

"The known, even though it wasn't good, was better than coming into a new school the last half of my senior year."

"You moved to Pinewood after leaving Sunview?"

Lily waved her hand. "We went farther south to Macon, which was a nice town, but everyone knew everybody, and I was the kid that no one was interested in befriending. I got a job at a local restaurant and spent most of my time there. My mother worked retail, and money was even tighter than when we lived in Sunview."

She rubbed the rim of her coffee cup. "After I graduated high school, we moved again and then again. I didn't realize my mother's memory was starting to fail. Turns out her blood sugar was out of control, and she had some other issues. Eventually, we went to Pinewood and moved in with my aunt. Two years ago, I decided to strike out on my own and started my taxi service along with working craft fairs."

"I'm sorry, Lily, that your childhood was so hard."

"Life isn't always easy, as you know too well."

"You said this is the first time you've come back to Sunview since high school?"

"That's right. If not for Pete Peterson, I might not have come back even after Betsy's letter, so maybe I should be grateful."

He raised his brow. "Why?"

"I wouldn't have met you and your family if it hadn't been for him."

Matthias's eyes darkened into an intense stare that made her heart lurch. Lily had spent her whole life keeping up her guard when it came to men. Here in the comfort of this Amish home, the walls she had built to protect her heart were starting to crumble.

She glanced down at Matthias's large calloused hands. He reached to take hers, but she shook her head. No doubt, he felt sorry for the teenage girl who had left town in the dark of night. As she had told the sheriff, she wasn't that girl anymore. She was a grown woman who could control her feelings and make a life for herself without a man.

Except, at the moment, with Matthias's gaze penetrating her heart, she didn't know what she wanted out of life. Surely, an Amish man would not be someone who could steal her heart.

"It's late." She scooted her chair back and stood. "I'll say good night."

He stood, stepped toward her and touched her arm. A spark of current traveled along her spine and curled around her neck. She let out a tiny gasp at his closeness before she pushed past him and hurried into the hallway, her heart pounding not from the exertion, but from the fear of what could have happened if she had remained in the kitchen. She didn't understand the way she felt and how quickly her equilibrium had been thrown into a tailspin. For a moment, a very long moment, she had thought about Matthias's hands pulling her into a close embrace. The mere thought had her pulse racing and her breath drawn.

Whatever was happening wasn't what she had planned for her life. She doubted Matthias had planned for an *Englisch* woman to stumble into his world, either. Lily wouldn't follow in her mother's footsteps. She couldn't give her heart to a man she had only just met. She wouldn't pull a family apart because she wanted to be loved and accepted, and she couldn't stand between a righteous man and the religion that guided his life.

Although she knew little about the Amish way, she knew the Amish didn't mix with the *Englisch*. She didn't belong in this home. Even more important, she didn't belong in Matthias's arms, no matter how much she wanted to be there.

Before she reached the door of the guest room, her cell phone rang. She glanced at the name on her screen: Baker. Her landlord.

"Hey, Mr. Baker. Is everything okay?"

"I have some bad news, Lily."

Her heartbeat picked up a notch. "Did something happen to my mother or Aunt Wilma?"

"Nothing like that. In fact, I called Wilma earlier, thinking you might be there, although I didn't mention the reason for my call."

"Is it something about the cabin?"

"A storm rolled in this evening. The lightning was heavy. I'm guessing a strike hit the propane tank and caused it to explode. A fire erupted." He paused for a long moment. "Looks like everything was destroyed."

She grabbed the doorjamb for support while Mr. Baker kept talking.

"The fire department is sending one of their investigators here tomorrow. The insurance company is dispatching an agent as well. I don't suppose you had renter's insurance?"

"Renter's insurance?" She shook her head, still unable to realize the significance of what he was saying. "No...no insurance."

"I hate that this happened, Lily. Look, I know it's late, but I wanted you to know as soon as possible."

"Thanks for calling."

"I'll be in touch. Let me know when you get back to this area. And, Lily..." He paused again. "I... I'm glad you weren't in the cabin tonight."

She disconnected and dropped the cell into her pocket, still unable to process what Mr. Baker had told her.

"Lily, is something wrong?"

She turned to see Matthias staring at her. "My…my plans have changed. I'd like to stay here a few more days, if that's all right?"

He looked confused. "That's good news, but are you sure you're okay?"

"My cabin—" She patted the pocket that held her cell phone. "My landlord called. Lightning… There was a fire. Everything's destroyed."

He was at her side in one fell swoop, holding her close and trying to comfort her.

"The cabin's withstood other lightning storms," she said between the tears that started to fall. "It wasn't an accident."

"What are you saying, Lily?"

"I'm saying that I'm sure somehow, someway, Pete Peterson set my cabin on fire."

Matthias remained at the kitchen table long after Lily had calmed down and gone to bed. She had still seemed in shock and claimed she would think more rationally in the morning. He, on the other hand, did his best thinking at night.

He mentally reviewed everything that had happened and how Peterson had tried to harm Lily time and time again. For what reason? For a flash drive? The three files didn't seem significant, and even the invoice provided no clue as to who had hired him and what his job entailed.

After pouring another cup of coffee, Matthias continued to mull over what they knew about Peterson, which wasn't much. Maybe he should take Lily's advice and wait until morning to sort things out.

He wished he could sort out his feelings for Lily as well. Truth be told, he was much too enamored with their houseguest. If he sought counsel, the bishop would tell him to ask her to leave his home. He would also tell Matthias to visit the widow Hochstetler, who the bishop claimed would make a fine wife and a loving mother to the children.

In the past, Matthias had explained that although thc widow was a nice person, she was not someone he wanted to have at his side for the rest of his life. The bishop had *tsked* and walked away as if Matthias were thinking of his own comforts instead of the well-being of his family.

Any friends Matthias confided in would also look askew at his interest in a non-Amish woman, and without a doubt, they'd offer to introduce him to their cousin once removed who lived in Ethridge, Tennessee, or Holmes County, Ohio, or perhaps Shipshewana.

His mother would not understand his confusion either. She enjoyed having Lily as a guest, but she would not want her to upset their Amish home.

As the cuckoo clock in the living room struck midnight, Matthias went outside to make sure no one was lurking nearby. Duke, his trusty sidekick, joined him, offering silent support and love. Even with Duke at his side, the cold night air did little to still Matthias's pounding heart or ease his confusion when he thought of Lily. Finally assured all was well on the farm, he returned to the house, locked the doors and climbed the stairs.

He slept little, and when he finally dozed off, he dreamed of a cabin engulfed in flames with Lily trapped inside. He woke in a cold sweat. The dream unsettled him even more than seeing her last night when she had been notified about her home. Had lightning been the cause, or was Lily correct in suspecting Peterson? The fire and insurance inspectors would eventually uncover the reason for the explosion and subsequent blaze. If Peterson was to blame, would their evaluation come in time to save Lily from being harmed again?

EIGHT

Matthias went outside the next morning and hurried through his chores, glad for the work to keep him occupied, although his mind remained on Lily. When he returned to the house, she was standing at the kitchen counter, pouring coffee.

She turned, her face drawn and her eyes red-rimmed as if she'd cried all night. His heart broke for her. He wanted to hold her close and tell her everything would be all right, but her house had burned, and a man was intent on doing her harm, so things weren't good. In fact, they were very, very troubling.

Lily handed him a cup of coffee, and their fingers touched for a moment longer than necessary. His mother entered the room and stopped, her lips pursed. Standing behind Lily, she raised her brow and stared at him as if to say her heart ached for Lily as well.

"I told your mother what happened."

Fannie patted Lily's arm. "And I told her she is welcome to stay here with us."

"You know that means so much to me, Fannie. Thank you, but I can't impose on your hospitality for too long."

His mother waved her hand. "Nonsense. Having you here is a joy. Besides, this gives you time to see your friend."

Lily nodded. "I finally got through to her this morning. She's been busy with a new job and didn't realize her voice mail was full. We arranged to meet later today." Her eyes brightened ever so slightly. "Betsy's working for Mrs. Lambert at the Christmas Lodge. She gets a lunch break and said she could meet me then."

Matthias worried about Lily's safety. "What if Peterson is there and he sees you?"

"Then I'll notify security and also the sheriff's office. I can't keep from living my life, Matthias."

"I know, but your safety comes first."

"What about taking the back roads to the lodge?" his mother suggested. "It is doubtful that someone who doesn't know this area would travel along those narrow paths."

"I think you've solved the problem, *Mamm*. We'll take the buggy. It won't be a fast trip, but you'll be out of sight in case Peterson is still in town. Although, if he was involved in the fire at your cabin, he might not be coming back to Sunview."

"I have a better idea, Matthias. If I follow you in my car, I can come back here and help Fannie this afternoon after Betsy returns to work."

The idea of spending at least part of the day with Lily made warmth spread through Matthias. It was the coffee, he told himself, but as he loaded his buggy with tools and decorations for the booth, he knew it wasn't the hot brew. It was Lily.

Whether he wanted to admit it or not. Her closeness, much as he liked it, was causing him to think of her as someone very special. He remembered his mother's warning about *Englisch* women who could steal a man's heart and shook his head. His foolish thoughts needed to stop. Maybe tomorrow. Maybe then he would have his fill of Lily and be ready to see her as a nice woman who did nothing to his heart.

At least, that was his hope.

But when she stood beside him as he arranged some of the items for sale in his buggy, he could smell the sweet scent of lavender and roses that hovered around her, and it made his neck tingle.

"Let's go over the route we're going to take to the lodge." He paused for a moment to look at her pretty blue eyes and thought of what could happen if Peterson saw her. "You've got to stay behind my buggy and on the dirt path. Keep checking behind your car and honk your horn if you see anything suspicious."

"I'll be okay, Matthias."

"We'll take a side road around Sunview, and another path that runs parallel to Mountain Road. Eventually, we'll turn onto Holly Trail as we near the lodge."

"I could probably use the GPS on my phone."

He shook his head. "I doubt they'd show these dirt roads. Only the old-timers and the local Amish farmers know they're there. If Peterson drives to the lodge, he'll take the main roads."

"Will there be a lot of people working on the various stalls?"

"*Yah*, the Amish sell their wares at the small booths at the side of the lodge. A few *Englisch* take part as well, but it is mainly Amish."

"The Keepers still own the lodge and Christmas store?"

"That's right. They're well-known and well-thought-of in the area. Three years ago, they invited some of the Amish craftsmen to sell their wares at the festival. Sales were good, and the Keepers get a commission on everything that sells, which was fine with the Amish. The number of booths has grown each year."

"Mrs. Keeper was a savvy entrepreneur, as I recall. My mother said she ran the lodge and was the reason it prospered. Mr. Keeper supported all her endeavors, but she was the brains of the operation."

"It seems that way," Matthias said. "Mr. Keeper's health has declined a bit since his daughter's death. He is still in his fifties, yet his gait has slowed, and his energy seems to have waned."

"I remember him being full of life. He was always happy to see me and made a point to make me feel welcome when I visited the lodge, even though my mother worked in housekeeping."

"A few Amish ladies work there now. Jobs at the lodge are sought-after."

"It used to be that the Keeper family took good care of their employees. Although I know that changed before my mother left, and I certainly have no idea what the working conditions are like now."

Lily glanced at the items in his buggy. "What about your furniture, Matthias? Will you sell some of your things there?"

He pointed to a three-ringed binder in one of the boxes. "I have a notebook with sketches of my work. People can place orders if they see something that strikes their fancy."

"I'm sure you'll make lots of sales."

Once the buggy was loaded, they said goodbye to Fannie and caravanned onto the road that passed in front of the farm. In less than a mile, they turned onto a narrow dirt road. Matthias flicked the reins and encouraged the mare into a lively trot. He kept looking back to ensure Lily was following close behind.

Before long, some of his anxiety lessened. Eventually, he saw the large sign at the turnoff to Holly Trail that welcomed them to the Christmas Lodge. Again, he glanced back. Lily stuck her hand out the open window and gave him a thumbs-up.

The forested entryway led to an expansive hillside with the grand four-story lodge at the top of the hill overlooking a fifty-some acre lake. The grounds were well-manicured, and festive signage directed visitors to the large Christmas shop located on the eastern side of the main building. A number of gazebos dotted the grassy knolls in each direction. An expansive porch wrapped around the lodge. Rocking chairs invited guests and visitors to relax, surrounded by festive Christmas wreaths and swags of evergreen, holly and twinkling lights that provided a festive mood even in the daytime.

Matthias pointed her toward the parking lot for automobiles before he guided his buggy to the rear of the property. After getting his mare settled, he hurried to join her.

Lily stepped out of her car and glanced around the property. "It's beautiful."

"Like you remember?" Matthias asked.

"Even more so." She smiled weakly. "Or maybe I'm older and can better appreciate the warmth and welcome that the lodge exudes."

"The Keepers work hard to ensure all visitors feel that aura of hospitality. Those of us manning the booths try to keep that same sense of wonder alive in our own small areas."

He pointed toward the distant pasture where he had left his buggy. "The Amish have an area farther from the lodge, but cars park in this first lot."

They grabbed tools and some decorating items out of her car, and Matthias led Lily to his booth. "From here, you can see the stage by the water where the show will occur tomorrow evening."

There was a hubbub of activity all around them. Matthias greeted a number of friends who were preparing their booths.

"Lily Hudson, is that you?"

Matthias turned as a pretty *Englisch* woman approached.

"It's been so long, but I'd recognize you anywhere," the woman continued.

Lily's eyes widened ever so slightly, then she smiled with recognition. "Janice Foster, how are you?"

The two women embraced.

"I wondered if you'd ever return to Sunview. I guess this year's festival has the drawing card of Clay coming back to perform."

"I heard he was going to be the main performer, but that didn't bring me back."

The other woman looked over at Matthias. He extended his hand, and she glanced at Lily as she accepted his handshake. "You two must be old friends."

"Actually, we met a couple days ago. I'm here to see Betsy."

Janice smiled slyly. "I heard she got a job at the lodge. By the way, did you know Kevin still lives in the area?"

Matthias watched Lily's expression sour. "Is he staying with his parents?"

Janice shook her head. "He owns land on Harper's Crossing on the west side of town. It's a big ranch he bought from Sharon Arnold's family. You remember her?"

Lily thought for a moment and then shook her head. "Actually, I don't recall her. It's been a few years."

"Of course it has. Plus, you were always busy working, and then you had to leave town so fast."

Lily bristled.

"Everyone knew your mother was innocent, even if Kevin spread those rumors."

"Rumors?"

Janice shrugged. "He was upset about his father having a thing for your mother. You knew that. He was so bitter."

"His parents are still together?"

"Yes." Janice blinked. "They are, but Kevin didn't realize at the time that they would reconcile."

She patted Lily's arm. "If I were you, I'd let Kevin know you're in town and explain how all that's in the past."

"I don't see any need to contact a person who spreads lies."

Janice shrugged. "Suit yourself, but if it were me, I'd want to ensure Kevin didn't bring up past history"

"He wasn't telling the truth."

Janice raised her brow. "Still, he could do damage. Stop by his house and tell him you didn't appreciate his comments. One thing about Kevin is he likes women who stand up for themselves."

"He was in love with Noelle. I never thought of her as being self-assertive."

"You're right, but he was in high school when he and Noelle dated."

"So he's changed?"

Janice sighed. "Maybe I was wrong about the

type of women he likes, but you can't let him continue to spread lies about you or your mother."

Lily seemed perplexed and more than unsettled.

"Perhaps he will come to the festival and you can talk to him here." Matthias offered the compromise as he searched around them, making sure Peterson wasn't in the crowd.

Lily evidently understood what he was saying. "I have to help Matthias. Good seeing you, Janice."

Together, they left Lily's high school classmate and headed to Matthias's semi-enclosed booth. It would provide more privacy and keep Lily somewhat hidden from the other vendors.

"Janice seems to know everyone's business," he murmured so only Lily could hear.

She nodded. "Which is exactly how she was in high school. I'm surprised she stopped to talk. We weren't friends in our teenage years. I always thought she looked down her nose at me because I came from the wrong side of town."

"The Amish do not think like you *Englisch*."

"No doubt because you have the love of God in your hearts. Not all *Englisch* think about social position, but regrettably, Janice did."

"She suggested you talk to Sheriff Granger's son."

"Which I might do after I talk to Betsy, but

I didn't want to give Janice anything more to gossip about. She likes to spread tales."

"Tall tales," Matthias added.

"Exactly." Lily placed the items she was carrying on the counter of the stall. "What can I help you with before I meet Betsy?"

"I want to shore up the sides of the booth. After a year in storage, it is good to make certain the stand can support the weight of the wares. Once I pound in the nails, I'll touch up the paint. It's a whitewash that goes on easily and is water-based."

He rooted through his supplies and found the can of paint and pried off the lid. "*Yah*, the paint is much too thick." He pointed to a small building that sat well to the rear of the lodge.

"The comfort station has water. I'll head there now."

Lily glanced at her watch. "You start nailing the stall together, and I'll get the water."

Matthias looked around the area, seeing mainly Amish folks. He didn't notice anyone with a limp or anyone wearing camo. "You need to stay in the booth where you're somewhat out of sight."

She studied the path to the comfort station. "Everything looks clear, Matthias." She glanced around. "Besides, Peterson would stand out in the crowd of Amish."

"Just as you do," he reminded her.

"I'll be careful."

Lily walked to the small building in the distance. Her hair blew in the breeze, and Matthias watched her until she rounded the building and disappeared from his sight.

Once again, he surveyed the Amish folks to make sure Peterson hadn't slipped into the mix before he reached for a jar of nails and his hammer. He enjoyed having Lily with him. She was easy to work with and agreeable, plus, she was pretty and being with her brightened his outlook. His mother would call him foolish, and perhaps she would be right. He would enjoy Lily's company for as long as she remained in Sunview, then he would go back to his former routine with his wonderful children and his mother. His family was everything to him, but he had to admit, Lily was a close second.

Lily entered the cabin-like structure and spied the sink and water spigot on the far wall situated near the restrooms. The common area was clean and had a couch and two chairs positioned around a coffee table. A large picture window looked out to a wooded area and provided a lovely backdrop to the comfort station where folks could stop to rest or wait for a friend or loved one using the facilities. A large wreath hung at the window, and the walls were decorated with various Christmas scenes. One showed children decorating a tree, another scene was of little ones building snowmen. In a third scene, people were skating on a frozen pond. Lily's heart warmed to the homey feel of the room and the lovely ornaments that hung from a small tree in the corner.

The Keepers thought of everything and tastefully decorated the entire property, including this rest station away from the main structure.

Lily unscrewed the top of the mason jar Matthias had given her, turned on the water and watched as the cool liquid flowed into the glass container. A sound alerted her that she wasn't alone just as the water reached the top of the jug.

She glanced over her shoulder.

All she saw was a blur of motion before a heavy weight crashed into her. The jar slipped from her hands, dropped into the sink and broke into tiny shards of glass.

"Augh!" she gasped.

A hand wrapped around her throat. Her knees went weak and she slumped to the floor, her head knocking against the sink as she fell.

"No." She grabbed his arm and tried to pry the man's fingers from her neck.

Out of the corner of her eye, she saw him. Dark eyes, scruffy beard, camo jacket.

Pete!

She kicked his shin and his grasp eased. She rolled away from him and scrambled to her feet.

He jabbed his fist into her stomach.

"Uff!" She doubled over, the air knocked from her lungs, and a wave of nausea rolled over her.

Gasping, she stumbled toward the door. He grabbed her shoulders and threw her to the floor.

"Where's the flash drive?"

Lily shook her head. He slapped the side of her face. The blow sent a jolt of pain down her spine. She whimpered, raised her hands to protect her face and kicked again.

He grabbed her leg. She jerked free and jammed her heel into his face. He fell backward, hands at his mouth. "Why you!"

She stumbled to her feet and lunged for the door just as it opened. An elderly woman stood in the threshold, eyes wide as she glanced from Lily to her attacker. The woman screamed.

Pete pushed past her, knocking the woman to the ground.

Lily raced to the woman's side. "Are you okay?"

"I… I think I'm all right." The older lady rubbed her forehead.

Through the open doorway, Lily saw Pete racing along one of the paths. He turned into a heavily wooded area and disappeared from sight.

The older woman's face was pale. Lily touched her neck and was relieved that her pulse was weak but steady. "What's your name, ma'am?"

"Eileen Turner."

"I'm Lily Hudson." She pulled out her phone, did a search for the Christmas Lodge and tapped the call icon.

"Merry Christmas from the Christmas Lodge. How may I direct your call?"

"Security."

A male voice answered on the second ring. "Christmas Lodge Security. Kyle speaking."

Lily briefly relayed what had happened. "An older lady named Eileen Turner needs medical attention, and the man who attacked both of us disappeared into the forested area. He needs to be apprehended."

"We'll be there in a matter of minutes."

Lily wanted to contact Matthias, but her first concern was for the older lady's well-being.

Two security guards dressed in navy uniforms, arrived on a golf cart. A nurse pulled up in a second cart right after them and checked Ms. Turner's vitals.

A woman dressed in a green skirt, white blouse and red sweater bearing the lodge logo joined them.

Lily recognized Alice Lambert, Clay's mother. "Mrs. Lambert."

"If it isn't Lily Hudson. I never thought I'd see you back at the lodge."

"Yes, ma'am. I'm here to see Betsy Wyler during her lunch break." She quickly explained about the man who had attacked her.

Mrs. Lambert wrung her hands. "I'll call Sheriff Granger, but we want this to be kept as quiet as possible. Adverse publicity could affect business."

Security took the woman to the first-aid station as Mrs. Lambert made the call.

"I hope Ms. Turner is going to be all right," Lily said once Mrs. Lambert disconnected.

"I'll check on her after I make sure you're okay." Mrs. Lambert eyed Lily. "You've got a scrape on your forehead and a red mark on your cheek."

"I'm all right, a little sore, but nothing's broken." She glanced at the lodge. "Where are Mr. and Mrs. Keeper?"

"In Atlanta picking up more holidays supplies. They should return later this evening."

"And you're in charge?"

"I'm in charge of activities." Her phone chirped and she stepped away to take the call.

"One of the sheriff's deputies will be here shortly," she told Lily after the call ended. "He wants to talk to you. Plus, I told security to let Betsy know what happened."

"Thank you."

"Of course." She patted Lily's hand. "Tell me, dear, how's your mother?"

"She's living in Pinewood with her sister. Some days are good, others are a struggle. She always liked you."

"And I liked her. I hate to think of her having problems."

Lily wouldn't mention that everything had been a problem after they had left Sunview.

"A lot happened about the time she stopped working at the lodge," Mrs. Lambert continued, "but I never believed what people said."

Lily tilted her head and raised her brow. "What did people say?"

"You know, dear, about your mother being involved. Kevin Granger spread some hateful rumors. No doubt, he was upset about his parents' rocky marriage. I understood that, although I'm not sure how many other folks saw through his comments."

"You mean he was spreading lies."

The woman smiled ruefully. "I'm sure your mother didn't kill Noelle. I would never think that."

Hearing her mother's name mixed with Noelle's death chilled Lily. Maybe both Janice and Betsy had been right. Lily needed to talk to Kevin Granger and make him realize Lily's mother had been with her the night Noelle died. They spent the night packing and getting ready to leave town. Lily could vouch for her mother. Whether Kevin would accept her alibi was the problem. But she needed to at least let it be known that Kevin was wrong and insist he stop spreading any more lies.

Lily glanced down, heavyhearted, then she heard her name as the door opened and Matthias raced inside.

"What happened?" he asked.

"Pete was here."

"Are you okay?"

She nodded, but she wasn't okay. She was worried about why Pete Peterson kept coming after her and why he wanted the flash drive. Was the invoice important? He didn't get paid until he completed the job, but did he need the invoice to collect his money?

"One of the sheriff's deputies will be here soon to get the information about what happened."

Matthias eyed her cheek. "He hit you."

"He wants the flash drive," she said when Mrs. Lambert stepped outside to flag down the deputy.

"Any idea why it's so important?"

"Maybe we should look at the files again."

"But you gave it to the sheriff."

"Remember I saved copies to my laptop and my phone." She still didn't trust Granger, even if it had been five years.

A lot had happened in the time she'd been away, but some people still thought her mother had something to do with Noelle's death. She needed to clear her mother's name, and she also wanted to see Pete apprehended for his crimes before she left Sunview—because once she left, she would never return again.

She glanced up at Matthias and realized that would mean never seeing him or his family again, and suddenly she wasn't sure of anything.

NINE

Matthias never should have asked Lily to get the water. He should have gone with her, or he should have left her at the booth where there were other people, instead of sending her to the remote comfort station.

Deputy Walker arrived and took her statement. Lily looked exhausted. It was no wonder after being accosted again. She claimed she hadn't been hurt, but Matthias knew she was holding back the seriousness of the attack.

Betsy arrived when the deputy was finishing his questioning. The two women hugged, and there was little doubt about the depth of their friendship.

Lily quickly filled Betsy in on everything that had happened.

"I feel terrible that you got hurt coming to meet me," her friend said. Betsy was about Lily's height with brown eyes and blond hair.

After the deputy left, Matthias suggested he

and Lily return to his farm, but she insisted he stay to get the booth ready for the next day.

"I won't let you drive home alone," Matthias said.

"With security and the sheriff's office searching for Peterson, he has to have fled far from here."

"You can't be certain of that."

"I'll stay on the same back road we took here. Pete would never think to look for me there."

Betsy glanced at her watch. "I've got about an hour of free time. Why don't I follow you at least to that road you mentioned, Lily?"

"You wouldn't mind?" she asked.

"Not at all. Matthias can get his work done, and you can get to his farm without a problem."

Matthias wasn't convinced it was the best idea, but Lily wanted to leave the lodge, and he had to finish shoring up the stall before tomorrow. He scanned the area for Pete. If Lily came back with him tomorrow for the festival, he would bring Duke to guard her, and he wouldn't send her off anywhere. A hard lesson learned.

More folks were arriving at the lodge, no doubt for the next day's festivities. Tomorrow, the stalls would open, carolers would sing at various times throughout the day and a parade would start in town and weave its way to the lodge for the evening program.

Matthias would give buggy rides, and children from the local schools would perform. After all the planning, he hoped the event would go off well, although his main concern and top priority was keeping Lily safe.

From what Deputy Walker had said, the sheriff's department would enhance security in the area and would remain vigilant for anyone matching Peterson's description. With the influx of visitors, Matthias wondered if one man would stand out from so many others dressed in outdoor attire. Pete's limp was a distinguishing characteristic, but even that would be difficult to spot in a crowd.

Lily grabbed her friend's hand. "Betsy, would you mind if we made a stop along the way?"

The request surprised Matthias. With her downcast face, he hadn't expected Lily to want to see anyone for the rest of the day. Then he realized what she needed to do.

"The sheriff's son?" he asked.

Lily nodded. "Kevin Granger." She turned to Betsy. "You mentioned him in your letter. Then Mrs. Lambert brought up the rumors he spread five years ago, and evidently, still brings up even now. I saw Janice earlier, and she said the same thing. Just as you wrote in your letter, I need to explain to Kevin that his comments are slanderous and untrue."

"That's a good idea," Betsy agreed. "Seeing him today before the festival might ensure he stops spreading those hateful lies."

"But will he listen?" Matthias asked.

"That's what I have to find out. He was a decent guy in high school. At least, until his father's interest in my mother became common knowledge."

"He and Noelle were going together," Betsy repeated what Lily had already told him.

"Was he ever considered a suspect in her death?" Matthias asked.

Betsy shook her head. "Not with his father investigating the crime. Kevin was given a free pass, as the saying goes. In fact, he was always considered a victim since his girlfriend was killed."

"Kevin made good grades and was a smart kid," Lily explained. "Unfortunately, he took his parents' separation hard, which is understandable."

Betsy's eyes widened. "Yet that doesn't give him the right to spread hate speech."

"Exactly." Lily nodded. "That's why I want to talk to him."

"He owns the old Arnold place on Harper's Crossing," Betsy said. "His house is just around the second bend."

"I don't like the idea of you talking to him alone," Matthias told Lily.

"I'll be with her," Betsy assured him. "Kevin may spread lies, but he would never hurt anyone. You don't have to worry. After we see Kevin, I'll follow Lily to that back road before I return to work."

"You'll let me know that Lily's safely on her way to the farm."

"I promise."

Matthias walked Lily to her car, and they waited until Betsy pulled up beside her. "Follow me, Lily. It shouldn't take us long."

Both women waved as they left the lodge property in the two cars. Matthias didn't like seeing Lily leave without him, but he had to work on the stall so they could open tomorrow for the festival. Both women had cell phones and would call Deputy Walker if there was a problem.

Matthias should feel relieved, but he knew anything could happen with Peterson on the loose.

Lily followed Betsy's car, grateful for her support.

Once they turned onto Harper's Crossing, Betsy pointed to the ranch house and carport in the distance and turned into the rather lengthy driveway. Lily parked next to her.

As Betsy got out of her car, her cell phone rang. She glanced at the screen. "It's Mrs. Lambert."

She lifted her cell to her ear and nodded a number of times. "Yes, ma'am. Certainly, that won't be a problem."

After disconnecting, Betsy looked at Lily. "I'm so sorry, Lily."

"She needs your help?"

Betsy nodded. "Will you be okay?"

"Of course, I'll be fine. I'm proud of you for snagging a job at the lodge. This won't take long, and I'll soon be headed back to Matthias's farm."

"He seems like a nice guy." Betsy smiled the same way she used to in high school when they were talking about cute boys.

Lily rolled her eyes. "Betsy, he's Amish."

"I know, but he's still handsome."

Lily had to agree.

She waved goodbye to Betsy and walked decisively to Kevin's front step. She hadn't expected to be nervous as she knocked on his door. She wasn't worried about her physical well-being, but digging up buried wounds wasn't easy. She would prefer to keep them hidden and out of sight. Still, after Janice, Mrs. Lambert and Betsy had commented that Kevin continued to spread rumors about her mother's involvement in Noelle's murder, Lily had to put a stop to the lies once and for all.

Gathering her courage, she lifted her hand to knock again. The door opened. Kevin stood on the threshold. His eyes widened as he recognized her. He was tall and muscular and still good-looking, although she saw a sadness in his eyes.

"What are you doing here?" His tone was full of vitriol.

"It's been five years, Kevin, but I understand you're still spreading rumors about my mother."

"Give it a rest, Lily."

She bristled. "How can I when you're convinced my mother was involved in Noelle's death."

"The facts are hard to refute."

"You don't know the facts. You jumped to conclusions that were false. I was with my mother that night. We were packing our car. In case you don't remember, we left Sunview twenty-four hours later."

"Which was convenient. I told my father to arrest you both and bring you back to stand trial for Noelle's murder."

"Your father knew we had nothing to do with her death."

"Someone saw your mother stop her car and talk to Noelle on a desolate back road that night. Your mother was the last person to see Noelle alive."

"I was in the car with my mother." The memory returned and brought with it the pain that Lily had lived with all these years. "My mother wanted to give Noelle a ride. She was cold, the road was dark and she shouldn't have been walking alone."

"Your mother heckled her."

"She did no such thing."

"Then why did she drive off in a huff?"

"Where are you getting your information? Noelle refused the ride and said she was meeting someone."

Lily stared at his narrow face and drawn eyes. Kevin was still grieving, or was something else going on? Had he, in some way, been involved with her death? "The last person who saw her alive was the person who murdered her," Lily said as she pulled in a breath and squared her shoulders. "Was that you, Kevin? Were you meeting Noelle that night?"

He pointed a finger at Lily, his eyes dark and seething with anger. "Get off my property. You weren't part of this town when you and your mother lived here, and you don't fit in now. Leave before something else happens."

"Are you threatening me?"

"And if I am, what are you going to do, tell the sheriff?"

"I'm sure he's aware his son has become a difficult person who sees the world through a vision of hate and bitterness."

"You don't know anything."

"I know about being in pain and not having anyone to turn to. You're eaten up with anger and frustration, Kevin. Are you mad at someone else or at yourself?"

"Aren't you being sanctimonious?"

"I'm being truthful."

"Here's what you don't understand, Lily. I don't want to see you again. As I mentioned earlier, get off my property."

She held up her hand to drive home her point. "Remember, Kevin, don't spread any more lies. If you're interested in what happened that night, ask me. I'll tell you everything I know, but don't make the situation worse."

"It couldn't get worse than Noelle dying." He pointed to her car. "Now leave me alone."

Tears burned Lily's eyes as she returned to her car. The memories of leaving town with people thinking her mother was involved in Noelle's death were like open wounds that still festered. She didn't know if she could ever forgive and forget, after the pain Kevin and his father had caused her mother.

Fannie would probably tell Lily to pray for both of them, but that was too much to ask of her. Someday, perhaps, the healing process would begin. Someday, but not now.

TEN

Matthias's pulse picked up a notch when he saw Betsy turn into the lodge driveway earlier than he had expected. "Is everything okay?" he asked, catching up to her.

"Lily's fine," she assured him. She held up her phone. "Mrs. Lambert called me back to work."

Matthias glanced around. "But where's Lily?"

"At Kevin's house. They'll probably have a long chat."

"Kevin Granger? The sheriff's son? She's alone with him?"

"Matthias, it's okay."

But it wasn't okay. He ran to his booth and locked the paneling so everything would be safe overnight. After asking the son of one of his Amish friends to drive his buggy home, he found a custodial worker getting ready to leave work and begged a ride to Harper's Crossing.

As grateful as he was for the man's help, Matthias didn't think he'd arrive there in time. He dropped a twenty-dollar bill onto the man's console as the custodian braked to a stop on the road in front of Kevin Granger's house. Lily was just backing out of the driveway. Matthias flagged her down and climbed into the passenger seat.

"You were worried," Lily stated the obvious.

"I thought you were taking the back roads home."

She sighed. "You knew I needed to talk to Kevin."

"But not alone. Betsy said she'd be with you."

What didn't Lily understand about staying safe? He hadn't heard her conversation with Kevin, but she appeared agitated, so it must not have gone well.

He knew that life could be unpredictable. When Rachel had delivered the twins, his joy had been hard to contain. Then in a short time, her condition had worsened. He and his mother had been focused on the babies and the chores that needed to be done. Rachel had assured them she was fine, and with the busyness of caring for the twins, he hadn't seen how pale she had become and how weak she was until—

He had raced to town to get the doctor, but medical help had arrived too late. His eyes burned with the memory, and his gut tightened.

He had begged *Gott* to save her, but his prayers had gone unanswered.

"*Gott*'s will," the bishop had intoned at her funeral, along with so many friends who offered that simple comment as if it could make everything right. For so long, Matthias hadn't known if anything could be right again. Slowly, he had returned to life, but his heart had continued to grieve. He had taken steps forward for his children, but not for himself.

A car's engine sounded behind them. Lily glanced at the rearview mirror. "Someone's approaching at a fast rate of speed."

He looked back and saw a white SUV. "Maybe there's an emergency."

"Maybe." She sounded doubtful. "How far are we from town?"

"A few miles at the most."

"He's not slowing down." Her hands tightened on the steering wheel. "Hold on, Matthias."

He swiveled around in the seat and stared at the driver. Due to the SUV's tinted windows, he couldn't get a clear view of the driver's face, but something told him it had to be Peterson. The car drew even closer.

"What's he doing, Matthias?"

Before he could answer, the SUV rammed into the rear of Lily's car.

The jolt jerked his head back. Lily gasped,

and her car careened onto the berm. She gripped the steering wheel, white-knuckled, steered back onto the main road and pushed down on the gas pedal. The car accelerated and started to shimmy.

"We're going too fast," she cried.

Matthias's pulse raced. "He's still behind us."

"I'm not sure the wheels will hold the road."

A sign warned of a sharp curve ahead. "Ease up on the gas, Lily."

She tapped the brake as they entered the turn.

The SUV started to pass them on the left. A deep gully edged both sides of the road.

"He'll force us into the ditch," Matthias warned.

Lily's eyes widened. Matthias followed her gaze, and his heart nearly stopped. A huge dump truck was headed into the curve in the oncoming lane. The truck driver laid on his horn. The deep sound blasted a warning.

The SUV swerved to escape a head-on collision. Tires screeched, and the truck driver raised his fist in anger. The SUV landed in the ditch.

Lily looked back. "Is he hurt? We need to help him."

"Don't stop. We'll notify the sheriff in town."

"But—"

"If it's Peterson, he has weapons, and he tried to kill you before. The sheriff can send someone to check on him."

"What does he want, Matthias?"

"Evidently, the flash drive is important, and he's willing to do anything to get it."

Even kill Lily. The thought made Matthias fist his hands. He had to protect her, but how could he keep her safe if he was supposed to follow a path of nonresistance?

Gott, help me, he prayed. *I have to keep Peterson from hurting Lily.* Matthias's blood chilled. He had to do more than that. He had to ensure Peterson didn't capture her in his crosshairs and shoot her dead.

Lily glanced over her shoulder and saw the white SUV angle back onto the pavement, turn onto a side road and disappear from sight. Peterson must not have been hurt too badly or he wouldn't have been able to drive away.

"He's on a farm road, Matthias. Why didn't he follow us?"

"I don't know." Matthias seemed as bewildered as she was.

"Does the farm road head into town?" Lily asked.

"It depends on whether he turns onto one of the narrow side spurs. They weave through the fields like a maze and a few lead to Sunview."

"Maybe he wants to head us off. We need to notify the sheriff."

The streets were filled with cars and buggies when Lily drove into town. "Folks must be going home from work."

Matthias nodded. "Plus, out-of-town visitors are here for the festival tomorrow."

"I wonder where Pete is staying? I told him about the lodge and the motel outside of town where I had planned to take him, although he wanted to go to Mountain Crest." She glanced at Matthias. "Any idea about the accommodations there?"

"There are two or three motels farther up the mountain."

She parked in front of the sheriff's office and hurried inside. Deputy Walker was at the counter.

"Miss Hudson, I didn't expect to see you this soon."

Lily explained what happened.

"Did he follow you from the lodge?" the deputy asked.

"Evidently," Lily said. "Although I thought you searched the area."

"We did. He might have been hiding in the woods."

Lily told the deputy about the near collision and the SUV trying to run her car off the road.

"Did the trucker stop?"

"He kept going."

"And you're sure Peterson was driving the SUV?"

"I didn't get a good look at his face, but he's the only one who keeps coming after me. It's got to be him."

"We'll search for a white SUV with possible damage to the front bumper. I thought you initially said you had given him a ride to town. Any idea where he got the car?"

"Is there a local rental car agency?"

The deputy shook his head. "Closest one is down the mountain, although there might be one in Mountain Crest. I'll check both locations. If either agency has recently rented a white SUV, we'll get the information and track down the drivers. Plus, I'll tell the rental agencies to notify us if anyone returns a vehicle with a dented front bumper."

"Have you inquired at the local hotels about a man matching Peterson's description?" Lily asked. "The limp should be a help."

"More men than you realize walk with a lopsided gait, but I called the motel on the road to town. They haven't seen anyone matching his description."

"What about Mountain Crest?"

"I'll check there next."

"And the B and B in Sunview?" she asked.

"I talked to Quin who was on duty last night."

Lily glanced at Matthias. "Maybe we should contact them today in case Pete's been hanging around."

"The sheriff should be back in the office shortly," the deputy assured them. "I'll tell him what happened when he returns."

Not that Sheriff Granger would do anything to help. He hadn't helped her mother in the past, and he hadn't been able to apprehend Peterson. Lily needed to take matters into her own hands, but she didn't know what to do, and she didn't know where to look. She closed her eyes for the briefest of moments.

God, I could use Your help!

ELEVEN

After leaving the sheriff's office, Lily followed Matthias across the street to a small gazebo where she tapped in the number to the B and B.

"Put your phone on speaker so we can both hear the clerk," Matthias said.

Lily complied with his request and held her cell out in front of her while the call connected.

"Hello there," a woman's voice rang out. "I'm Cynthia Nichols, the owner of the Sunview B and B. If you're inquiring about a room, we have a couple openings for tonight, but we're booked for the rest of the week."

Lily introduced herself and went on to explain about the incident last night. "The man who was peering through the window goes by the name of Pete Peterson, although he could be using an alias."

The owner pulled in a sharp breath. "I'm sorry about what happened and am relieved you weren't hurt in any way. Truth be told, I've been a bit on edge today, wondering if he would return."

"That's why I'm calling." Lily glanced at Matthias. "Peterson's about six feet tall, walks with a limp and has long hair and a beard. Every time I've seen him, he's been dressed in a camouflage jacket and dark cargo pants. Have you noticed anyone matching that description?"

"Thankfully, no. All our current guests are married couples, and no one has a problem walking."

Lily rattled off her cell number. "If you see anyone who fits his description, would you call me or the sheriff's office?"

"Certainly. I'll call the sheriff's office immediately."

Grateful for the woman's help, Lily disconnected. "At least, we know he's not staying at the B and B."

Matthias nodded. "After what happened last night, I'm convinced Cynthia will keep an eye out for him."

He glanced back at the sheriff's office. "I'll tell Deputy Walker that we contacted the B and B and meet you at the car."

As Matthias entered the sheriff's office, Lily crossed the street. A woman came out of what appeared to be a trendy boutique. She was tall and slender with long honey-brown hair, dangling earrings and a matching sweater and slacks outfit.

Lily recognized Roxanne Granger, the sheriff's wife. Not wanting to be noticed, Lily lowered her gaze, but before she could get to her car, she heard the woman call her name.

"Lily Hudson, what are you doing back in town?"

She wanted to ignore the comment, but Lily and her mother had run away from Sunview once; she wouldn't let anyone, even the sheriff's wife, make her flee again.

"I'll ask you one more time," Roxanne Granger demanded, her voice raised. "Why are you in Sunview?"

Lily turned toward the woman and tried to smile in greeting, although she knew her expression was anything but sincere. "Hello, Mrs. Granger."

"Tell your mother she's not welcome in town."

"My mother isn't here."

The woman pursed her thin lips. "I don't believe you."

"That's your choice, but you have no say as to whether she or I come back to Sunview."

"Except for a murder case that could be reopened."

"I've already talked to Sheriff Granger. He's aware of why I'm here."

"He didn't mention it to me." Mrs. Granger huffed.

"My mother and I pose no threat to you or your husband. Five years have passed." She thought of Fannie's words. *You need to live in the present instead of dwelling on the past.*

"Who do you think you are to talk like that to me?"

"Ma'am, I meant no disrespect."

"That's absurd. Of course, you did. You and your kind are always disrespectful."

Lily felt a tug at her heart. "I'm not sure what you mean by *my kind.* If you're referring to a woman raised by a single mother who worked hard to make ends meet, I see nothing disrespectful or negative in that."

"Your mother tried to break up my marriage."

"My mother wasn't the only person involved."

"How dare you speak to me like that!"

A man came out of the store where Mrs. Granger had been shopping. "Is there a problem, Roxanne?" he asked.

The sheriff's wife pointed to Lily. "She's the problem."

A few people took out their cell phones and started to record the incident.

The shopkeeper glanced at Lily. "We don't want any trouble in Sunview."

Lily squared her shoulders. "Perhaps you

should direct your comment to Mrs. Granger then."

The store clerk didn't appear happy with her comeback. "Young lady, it would be best if you get in your car and drive away."

"Because Mrs. Granger doesn't want me here?"

He seemed flummoxed. "Sunview is a peaceful city."

"Not when there's a murderer in town." The sheriff's wife pointed to Lily.

A number of people gasped. More cameras turned on Lily. The memory of being ostracized in her youth washed over her again.

A crowd of people had gathered on the street, blocking her from accessing her car. Her cheeks burned and a lump filled her throat, but she wouldn't let Mrs. Granger see her cry. She glanced at the sheriff's office, hoping to see Matthias, but he was nowhere in sight, and an even larger crowd blocked the road in that direction.

"If you'll excuse me." Lily kept her head high and her shoulders back. She crossed the street and entered the restaurant where she had worked as a teen. The waitress on duty was gathering an order from the kitchen and didn't notice Lily. Some of the patrons glanced up as she passed their tables on the way to the rear hallway where the restrooms were located. Instead of going into the ladies' room, she exited the restaurant through the back door that led to the alley.

Once outside and away from the gawking crowd, Lily breathed in a lungful of cool, crisp air, brushed the tears from the corners of her eyes and headed to the park to wait for a few minutes until the crowd on the street dispersed. Then she could make her way to the sheriff's office, where she hoped to find Matthias, who was no doubt still talking to the deputy. She hated that she'd run off, but she could no longer take the jeers from the people gathered around Mrs. Granger.

Lily entered the park and settled onto a bench under an oak tree. Dropping her head into her hands, she inhaled deeply in an attempt to catch her breath and get control of her erratic heartbeat and even more erratic emotions.

The sound of a car driving by caused her to glance up. A white SUV. Her heart lurched and her pulse raced. The car slowed to a stop and parked at the curb. Continuing to focus on the vehicle, she quickly backed onto one of the paths.

The driver's door opened and a man stepped to the pavement. He rounded the car, stared at her for a long moment and smirked.

Pete!

She turned and ran. The path led through a cluster of trees that hid her from the road. Lily recognized the area from her youth, but so much had changed and she was confused by a series of paths that came together ahead. Unsure which one would lead back to the downtown area, she veered right.

Footsteps sounded behind her. She was afraid to turn around. It had to be him.

She left the path and ran through a stand of trees. If only she could find Matthias.

A hand grabbed her. She tripped and fell to her knees. "Umph!"

"You're always running away from me."

She glanced over her shoulder at Pete's snarl, and her chest tightened. "What do you want?" she demanded.

"Where's the flash drive?"

If Lily told Peterson that the sheriff had the flash drive, she would no longer be of use to him and feared he'd be even more enraged. She thought of Cynthia Nelson's assurance she would call the sheriff if she saw anyone matching Peterson's description and knew that was her only hope of surviving.

"The flash drive's in my room at the B and B." Lily scrambled to her feet and pointed to a nearby path. "I'll get it for you."

"No, you don't, little lady. You're not going

anywhere alone." He grabbed her arm and twisted it behind her back.

She grimaced with pain. "Let me go."

"You're staying with me. We'll walk there together."

He shoved her through another cluster of trees. She could see people in the distance.

"Help me!" Lily screamed, trying to get someone's attention.

One man looked up, but he ignored her cry.

Something hard jammed into her side. "One more word, and you'll never talk again."

"You wouldn't shoot me in the middle of town."

He snarled. "Don't tempt me."

"Why's the flash drive so important?"

"Shut up and keep walking."

"It has to do with the lodge, right? Are you staying there?"

"I said shut up."

"The sheriff will find you."

He yanked her arm higher, and dug the nozzle of the gun deeper into her back. In the distance, she spied the B and B.

At that moment, he pushed her into a deserted alleyway. The sour smell of rotting refuse assailed her as they passed a dumpster and a row of garbage cans.

A cat peered into a discarded box of trash. A long-tailed rodent jumped out and skittered around the side of the building and the cat chased after it.

Lily was being held by another rat, and she needed to use her head to get away from him. Yet, no matter how hard she tried, she couldn't think of any way to escape.

"God, help me," she moaned silently.

"Quiet." His breath fanned her neck. "Do what I say and you'll live. One slipup, and you'll be dead."

Matthias couldn't find Lily. He had pushed through the crowd on the sidewalk in time to see her enter the café. He hurried through the restaurant and raced down one alleyway and then another.

Where is she?

His ears rang, and he felt like a wild animal trapped in a maze.

"Lily?" He stopped to listen, but the only sound was a car passing on the street and the *clip-clop* of horses' hooves in the distance.

He ran through the park, his heart pounding with fear, and then angled back toward the main part of town. The sheriff's department came into view. He barged inside and headed straight for the sheriff's office. Instead of knocking, he pushed open the door. The sheriff blanched, his eyes wide with surprise, and he reached for his weapon.

Matthias held up his hands. "Lily's disappeared. Your wife was badgering her."

"My wife?"

"On the street. Lily fled into the café. By the time I got there, she was gone. Someone said she ran out the back door."

"Where's my wife?"

"I presume she went home."

The sheriff groaned. "Let's go."

On the way through the office, Granger called to his deputy on duty. "Send out an alert. We need to canvas town for Lily Hudson. That Peterson guy is still on the loose."

"I just heard back from the last of the motels in Mountain Crest. No one there meets Peterson's description."

"Because he's still in Sunview," the sheriff lamented.

Matthias's gut tightened.

The phone rang and the sheriff answered. "Granger." He listened for a long moment and then nodded. "Roger that."

His face was tight when he disconnected. "The owner of the B and B said someone's trying to get in her back door. She said there's a frightened woman being held by a man in a camo jacket."

Matthias ran faster than the sheriff. He had to get to Lily before Peterson harmed her. Why had he told her to meet him at the car while he talked to Deputy Walker? Peterson had grabbed her, and Matthias couldn't bear to think of what could happened.

"Stay back," the sheriff warned. "You don't want to get hurt."

Matthias didn't care about his own well-being. All he could think about was Lily. He raced around the corner of the alleyway and saw her. He also saw the man holding a gun to her head.

"Lily," Matthias screamed.

"Drop the weapon." The sheriff came to a stop next to him. "Let the woman go."

Everything happened in a whirl.

Peterson fired at them and backed into an intersecting alleyway, all while holding Lily in front of him like a shield. Once he rounded the corner, he shoved her aside and ran.

The sheriff called into his radio. "Head him off. He's on his way to the park."

Sirens sounded in the distance, and the sheriff raced ahead. Matthias dropped to his knees next to Lily. Her face was pale, and her lips trembled. Confusion clouded her eyes for a moment before she reached out and held onto him as if her life depended on him.

But he had failed her.

The sheriff would find Peterson, and everything would be over, yet Matthias would always remember not being able to keep Lily safe. The terrible sick feeling of losing Rachel returned, only this time he was worried about losing the precious woman crying in his arms.

What was wrong with him? Lily could have died today, and he hadn't been able to save her.

TWELVE

Lily couldn't stop trembling. The sheriff had taken her statement, starting with his wife's hateful remarks.

"Roxanne never should have accosted you on the street, Lily. I'm sorry about her actions."

"I needed to get away from the growing crowd of onlookers and their cell phones. The park seemed like the best place to regroup, but Peterson saw me."

"If you're able to drive, I suggest you get to Matthias's farm before nightfall. Lock the doors. Be on guard. You still have your cell, right?"

She nodded.

"Keep your car out of sight, and call me if you see anything out of the ordinary. I'll let you know when we apprehend him."

Lily didn't share the sheriff's optimism. She said little on the way home and was grateful that Matthias didn't try to engage her in conversation. She felt a sense of relief once she turned into their drive and parked in the barn. Matthias's mare was there, along with his buggy.

Fannie greeted her, and from her expression, Lily knew the older woman realized something was wrong.

"The children are not home yet, and I've been worried since a neighbor brought Matthias's buggy home. Come sit at the table and tell me what happened. I'll make you a cup of tea."

Lily explained about Mrs. Granger and her run-in with Peterson.

"School will end soon," Matthias said after looking at the wall clock. "I'll take the buggy and get the children. Why don't you rest while I'm gone, Lily."

She shook her head. "I don't need to rest, but I need to wash my hands and face so the children don't see the dirt smudges."

Matthias squeezed her hand before he left. "Remember to lock the kitchen door behind me."

Fannie noticed the way he looked at her and pursed her lips, which unsettled Lily even more. What was she doing to this good Amish man and to his family? She had brought danger to their doorsteps, and she was upsetting their peaceful existence. She would never be able to forgive herself if Matthias or his mother or most especially his children were hurt.

After thanking Fannie for the tea and for her concern, Lily went into the guest room. She closed the door and then sat on the bed, head in her hands, trying to work through everything that had happened.

Once again, Peterson had come after her. He wanted the flash drive for whatever reason. Surely, it wasn't the invoice or the Christmas Lodge brochure. The only other file of interest was the graphic of converging lines. Why would that be important to him?

She pulled in a breath and steeled her resolve. She was determined to stay in Sunview. Mrs. Granger and her son wouldn't force her away. Neither would Peterson, even if he remained on the loose. She wouldn't let him win. She had to take control of her own life, which is what she had done after leaving her aunt's house two years ago. She'd made her own way and created her own life, and she'd endured. She had done it then, and she would do it now. No one would force her to leave Sunview until she was ready. Or until Matthias said she needed to go.

The children were exuberant on the drive home from school and eager to see Lily. "She really is *gut* with jacks, *Datt*," Sarah exclaimed. "I hope we can play again tonight."

"Miss Lily might need to rest this evening.

We had a busy day getting the booth ready for the Christmas festival," he told the children. "The parade's tomorrow afternoon."

"Last year, Duke went with us," Toby reminded him.

"He can join us again this year," Matthias assured his son. Duke was a *gut* watchdog and would offer protection if Peterson appeared again.

"When you go into the house, try to be quiet in case Lily is resting."

"Is she sick?" Sarah asked.

"I don't think so, but we need to ensure she gets her rest."

"I told our teacher about our houseguest."

Matthias wondered what the schoolmarm thought about an *Englisch* woman staying with his family.

"She said Miss Lily must be a very nice lady if our *Mammi* has invited her to stay."

Matthias had a hard time not snickering. Evidently, the children's teacher was well aware of his mother's struggle with the *Englisch*.

Upon arriving home, he reminded the children once again to go inside quietly. He unhitched the mare and groomed and fed her before he went inside. To his surprise, he found Lily sitting at the kitchen table. Sarah sat on her left and Toby on her right. Their sweet heads were bent over their schoolwork. Lily glanced up.

She had washed her face and pulled her hair into a bun at the nape of her neck. Her eyes were heavy, but she had changed into a fresh blouse and attempted to smile when he entered the kitchen.

"I'm glad everyone's working on homework." He wiped his feet on the small rug just inside the door.

"We will eat as soon as the children finish their lessons," his mother announced. She pulled a beef roast surrounded by potatoes and carrots from the oven. The rich smell filled the house along with the aroma of fresh bread she had baked earlier today.

"Sarah is finishing her last math problem." Lily glanced at Toby's paper. "And Toby is writing the concluding sentence in his short story."

"It is about an Amish boy who lost his dog and thought he would never find another dog to love." He glanced at Lily out of the corner of his eye. His cheeks pinked. "Then a stray appeared at his door. The new dog didn't take the old dog's place, but they became friends, and that helped the boy feel less sad about losing his old dog."

"That's a lovely story, Toby." Lily rubbed her hand over the boy's shoulder. "With a good lesson about love. Remember we talked about how love begets love, and that love comes from God."

"*Gott* loves everyone," Sarah stated before she handed Lily her paper. "Will you check my last two problems?"

Lily studied the paper and then smiled. "Good job. You got them right."

"Clear the table if you are finished with your lessons," Fannie said to the children. "Then wash your hands and set the table."

"I'm glad you're here." Sarah grabbed Lily's hand.

Matthias was touched by the attention Lily gave his children and equally touched by the story Toby had written. Was he trying to express the way he felt about Lily and the special place he had in his heart for the newcomer who had stumbled into their lives?

"Can we play games after dinner?" Toby asked.

"It depends upon what your father says." Fannie glanced at him.

Toby looked pleadingly at Matthias. "Please, *Datt*."

"After we help *Mammi* with the dishes and get them back to the cupboard, there should be time for a few games."

"Jacks," Sarah announced.

"Pick-up sticks," Toby declared.

"What about dominoes?" Fannie suggested with a twinkle in her eye.

"*Mammi*, will you play, too?"

His mother nodded. "When the work is done."

Matthias couldn't remember his mother ever taking time to play a game in the evening. His father would play checkers with Matthias and sometimes chess, but his mother always had mending to do or some other chore that needed her attention.

He glanced at Lily. She seemed to be a *gut* influence on all of them.

In spite of everything that had happened, there was a lighthearted joviality around the dining table as they ate. Perhaps the adults were putting on a facade for the children, but it felt good. The levity continued as they all joined in a game of dominos that took far longer than they had expected. His mother's throaty laugh filled the house and added to the enjoyment of the evening.

Once the game was over and the children were tucked into bed, his mother retired to her room. Lily and Matthias refreshed their cups of coffee and stepped onto the porch.

Lily leaned against the railing and stared into the night sky. "There are so many stars."

"That's the advantage of living far from town. Out here, we can see the sky studded with twinkling lights. The constellations are easy to pick out."

"Oh, there." Lily pointed to a meteor falling through the sky. "It's a shooting star." She glanced at Matthias. "Did you make a wish?"

"Is that an *Englisch* custom?"

She shrugged. "It's something I did as a child."

"Then I'll make a wish."

Matthias closed his eyes and then blinked them open to see Lily with her eyes closed and her face in deep concentration.

She opened her eyes, and the look in her gaze made his heart lurch. The night was quiet, and cold air wrapped around them and drew them one to another. She leaned into him, and he smelled the fresh scent of her hair, a mix of lemon, lavender and a hint of rose petals.

He stopped thinking about what might keep them apart and thought only of Lily's nearness and his desire to feel her warmth and the softness of her wrapped in his arms. He leaned closer, and his eyes focused on her sweet mouth that he wanted to kiss. His pulse raced with anticipation as their lips touched, and his heart nearly exploded.

"Lily." The kitchen door opened, and his mother stood on the threshold. "Your phone is ringing."

Lily's gaze was filled with confusion. Her lips looked swollen, and her face was drawn in disappointment. Perhaps she too had wanted their kiss to last longer.

He stepped back and let her pass as she hurried inside. His heart ached at the separation. He glanced at the night sky, and another shooting star appeared above him.

Did you make a wish? Lily's words played back to him.

His wish? That Lily were Amish. Then the feelings he had for her could be realized.

"Matthias, it is cold outside. Come into the house."

"Yah." He appreciated his mother's concern for his well-being, but he wanted to remain on the porch in hopes Lily would return, even though they could not allow their emotions to have free rein again. He had made a mistake by kissing her, yet the memory would remain with him throughout the night as he remembered the way she felt in his arms.

He stepped into the kitchen and glanced into the living room where she held the phone to her ear.

"Thank you, Sheriff. I'm relieved."

She disconnected and turned to face him. "Pete was seen at a local bar, although he gave the bartender another name. He was wearing a camo jacket and was seen leaving the place in a white SUV and driving somewhat erratically. The sheriff's eager to get him off the road lest someone get hurt."

"This is *gut,*" Fannie said.

Lily nodded. "It means soon we won't have to worry."

"If they apprehend him, and if it is Peterson," Matthias cautioned.

"You don't think it's him?" Lily asked.

"I don't think a hired killer would be so foolish to drive while intoxicated."

"You can stop at the jail tomorrow and identify him," Fannie suggested.

Lily nodded. "Although I don't want to see him again."

"But you must."

"I know." She sighed and glanced at the wall clock. "I'm going to get some sleep. Maybe all of this will be resolved by morning. Right now, I'm not sure what tomorrow will hold."

Once Lily retired to her room, Matthias walked outside again and stared into the night sky, wishing he could turn back time and go back to when he had Lily in his arms. A foolish thought, and so unlike him. He needed to focus on the festival. There was much to do, yet right now, he could only think of Lily.

THIRTEEN

Lily awoke before dawn. She dressed quickly and hurried downstairs to where Fannie was already fixing breakfast.

"The coffee's hot." The older woman pointed to the pot. "I just poured a cup for myself."

Lily glanced at the biscuits Fannie was ready to place in the oven. "Every day, you get up early to cook for Matthias and the children."

Fannie nodded. "*Yah*, this I have done my entire life."

Lily stared through the window into the blackness. The oil lamps brightened the kitchen, but the sky through the window was still dark. She could see the morning star hanging low in the sky.

"What can I do to help?"

"The children need lunches packed. If you could make sandwiches. Peanut butter and jam is a favorite. Make them with the biscuits you fixed last night."

"And your homemade jam?"

"Our strawberries were plentiful this year, and the jam is their favorite."

Lily made the sandwiches and put them in the lunch boxes, along with homemade cookies and a small apple for each child.

"I don't like to pry." Fannie pursed her lips. "Is there a special man in your life? Have you ever thought of getting married?"

Lily was surprised by the questions. "No boyfriend, and before I think of marriage, I need to fall in love."

Fannie nodded. "*Yah*, love is important, but love grows with time."

"Either way, I'm still working to earn money for my mother's care. Now that my cabin is gone, I'll have a lot of necessities to buy."

"These days without work cost you."

"If the Christmas festival is successful, I may be able to make up for a portion of what I've lost in my taxi business. Plus, I might make contacts for future craft fairs."

"The one at the Christmas Lodge is the biggest in the area. The children will be released early from school today. I will pick them up in our smaller buggy, and we'll drive to the lodge to join in the fun. It would be a relief if Peterson has been arrested."

"The sheriff sent a text message to me last

night, Fannie, confirming he had apprehended Peterson. Plus, according to what I heard yesterday, the sheriff and the lodge have increased security. I'm certain the Keepers will be at the festival, ensuring everyone remains safe."

"Mrs. Keeper oversees all the details, although Clay Lambert's mother handles a lot on the business end."

"Her son has a wonderful voice and has become quite a star."

"It is *gut* he can come back to perform. There will be a parade. Some of the Amish men provide buggy rides for the families." She raised her brow. "You will be there, *yah*?"

"If you don't mind me staying another night."

"You know we enjoy your company. Besides, where would you go if you leave?"

"My aunt will let me sleep on her couch. I need to go back to driving my taxi, especially if Pete Peterson is in jail."

"What are you saying?" Matthias asked as he entered the kitchen, bringing the cool morning air along with him.

Lily explained about the text message from the sheriff.

His face brightened with the news.

Fannie turned back to her oven. "How early are you leaving for town today, Matthias?"

"Right after breakfast," he told his mother.

"Lily probably needs to stop at the sheriff's office to identify Peterson before we go to the lodge."

Fannie nodded. "Even with Peterson in jail, I worry about Lily's safety after everything that has happened. Plus, I do not trust the sheriff. Virtue eludes him. For all we know, he could release Peterson on a technicality." She raised her finger to her forehead. "But *Gott* tells us to use the intelligence He gave us to outsmart the world, *yah*?"

Lily nodded. "Outsmarting Peterson is what I've been trying to do."

"And you have succeeded thus far." She smiled at Lily. "But for such an important day, have you thought of changing your appearance slightly so you would be less recognizable?"

Lily glanced at Matthias, hoping he could explain what his mother was referencing. He shook her head ever so slightly, and Lily turned her gaze back to Fannie.

"Are you saying I should wear a costume when I'm at the festival?" She pointed to Matthias. "Perhaps dress like a man so I can go unnoticed?"

Fannie laughed. "How could a lovely lady like you pass for a man?" She shook her head. "You should not try to be a man. Instead, you should become an Amish woman."

"But how would that change my appearance?"

"Dressed like an Amish woman with your hair in a bun and a *kapp* on your pretty hair, this Mr. Peterson would not suspect you to be the taxi driver he is seeking who usually wears jeans and sweaters."

"He might have seen me with Matthias."

"If so, you were dressed *Englisch*. He will not think to look for you among the many Amish women at the festival."

"And where could I get Amish clothing this morning when we're leaving for town so soon?"

Fannie turned to Matthias and said something to him in Pennsylvania Dutch. He thought for a moment and nodded.

"Do you mind translating?" Lily asked.

"There are dresses packed away upstairs," the older woman said. "They would fit you, I feel sure, and we could readjust the pins if needed. I have a new *kapp* that will cover your bun, as well as a black cape and larger bonnet to wear outside."

"But—"

"My mother is right, Lily." Matthias stepped closer. "If Peterson should still be on the loose, he will not recognize you as an Amish woman. He will be searching for his taxi driver. You can watch for him, and we can notify security at the lodge if you see anyone who fits his description."

"I will get the clothing from the trunk." Fannie climbed the stairs, leaving Lily to stare at Matthias. She realized to whom the Amish clothing had belonged, and her heart went out to him.

"Your mother asked if I could wear Rachel's clothing."

He nodded. "She wanted me to make the decision."

"I don't want to do something that will hurt you, Matthias."

"Keeping you safe is what is important. Rachel has been gone for seven years now. It is time for me to focus on the present instead of the past."

"But there will be too many memories."

He touched his heart. "I have kept the memories here. That will not change, but seeing you in her clothing will put the clothing to *gut* use. There is no reason they should remain unworn."

"Are you sure?"

"As the children say—" he touched his chest "—cross my heart."

"Oh, Matthias." She couldn't think of a way to convince him that this wasn't a good idea. "I don't want to bring you more pain."

"You, Lily—" he stepped closer and rubbed her cheek "—you could not bring me pain."

Something burned in his eyes, and she gasped at the way his gaze warmed her neck. He leaned toward her. Her heart slowed, and everything went quiet. All she could see was Matthias and his lips lowering to—

Her phone chirped. She closed her eyes for a moment, wishing her cell would stop ringing.

Fannie's footsteps sounded on the stairway. "I just woke the children." She stopped and listened. "Do you hear your phone, Lily?"

Lily stepped away from Matthias and dug in her pocket. She accepted the call and raised the phone to her ear.

"This is Sheriff Granger. Turns out the man we apprehended yesterday had someone to vouch for him. He and his sister have been caring for his elderly mother for the last week and never left his mother's bedside. His name's McAlister. He's a local guy, evidently well-liked, although he hits the sauce a little too heavily at times. We let him go this morning. It seems Pete Peterson could still be in the area, which means I'll need your help at the festival. You're the only one who can identify him in case he decides to cause trouble. I'll let you know if anything develops on my end, and we'll connect this afternoon after the parade."

Fannie had been right. Peterson wasn't in jail.

"And, Lily—"

"What is it, Sheriff?"

"I'm sorry about hurting your mother. My marriage was rocky, and Violet made me think of how much better my life could have been."

Lily didn't know whether to be angry or sad. "Maybe you should have thought of my mother's feelings instead of your own."

After disconnecting, she glanced at Matthias. "The sheriff had the wrong man. Peterson is still on the loose." She turned to Fannie. "I'll wear the Amish clothing today and keep my eyes open for anyone who could be Peterson. He could try to hide his identity as well."

"Then perhaps you should stay here and not attend the festival," Fannie cautioned.

"But I'm the only one who can identify him."

"Still, I'm worried about you, dear."

"Matthias will be with me." Yet, he looked worried, too.

Fannie let out a heavy sigh and handed Lily the clothing she had in her arms. "Then it is decided. You can change after breakfast."

"I'll take the children to school before we go to the Christmas Lodge." Matthias's face was drawn.

"What will Sarah and Toby think about me wearing their mother's clothing?"

"First of all, they never knew their mother," Matthias reminded her. "And they certainly won't recognize her clothing. We'll tell them you wanted to dress Amish while you work at the Christmas Lodge. It won't be a problem."

But Lily felt like it would be. She felt like she was a problem. She had interfered with Matthias's life and sent everyone into a bit of a tailspin, which wasn't what she had wanted to do.

With a heavy sigh, she hurried to the guest room and changed into the Amish dress. Pinning the fabric was more of a challenge than she had expected, and she was grateful when Fannie tapped on her door.

"Breakfast is ready," the older woman stated and peered into the room. "I thought you might need help."

"You must have read my mind. I'm struggling with the straight pins."

Fannie nodded. "They are a challenge, for certain." She readjusted the pins Lily had already used and then slipped a few more into the waistband. "There," Fannie said once the job was done. "Now you must do your hair and *kapp*."

Together, they brushed Lily's hair into a bun, secured it with hairpins and did the same with the *kapp*.

"It's so light," Lily said once the *kapp* was in place.

"Amish women cover their heads when they

pray. We wear the *kapp* so we can pray at any time throughout the day."

Lily lowered her gaze. "I hate to admit that prayer is not something I do regularly."

"*Gott* is with you whether you pray or not. However, He wants us to get to know Him better, and prayer is the way to deepen our relationship with Him."

"I fear He has given up on me."

Fannie shook her head. "*Gott* never gives up on us. We are the ones who walk away from Him, but He has His arms open wide, ready for when we come back to Him. It is never too late."

Lily thought of her life, of the confusion of her youth and her dysfunctional mother who never could find happiness. Had God been with them during all those years of struggle?

If what Fannie said was true, maybe Lily needed to reach out to the Lord more and try to develop a relationship with Him.

Lily followed the older woman into the kitchen. The children were pouring milk into their glasses. Matthias was the first to see her. The color in his face drained as he glanced at the dress she wore. Evidently, she had upset him, just as she'd worried she would.

"You look very pretty," Sarah said as she took her glass to the table.

Toby said nothing, but the sweet smile on the

boy's cherub face let her know that he approved of her outfit.

Unable to look squarely at Matthias, Lily carried the coffeepot from the stove to the table and filled the mugs for the three adults.

As she hurried back to help Fannie plate the food, Matthias caught her hand. She glanced at him, feeling her cheeks warm. The color had returned to his face, and he stared at her with the same intense gaze that had taken her by surprise last night.

"That shade of blue suits you, Lily."

"*Danki*, Matthias. The dress is lovely. I'm sure Rachel was a wonderful seamstress as well as a steadfast wife."

"She was." He nodded. "But each person has their own attributes, and yours are equally as important."

He squeezed her hand for reassurance before she returned the coffeepot to the stove and carried the filled plates to the table.

As they sat for the morning meal, Matthias, Fannie and the children lowered their heads. Lily did as well, but she didn't give thanks for the food. She gave thanks for this lovely family who had allowed her to enter into their world if only for a few days. She felt a deep connection with all of them and wished, for a moment, that she would not have to leave them.

Then she sighed, realizing her foolishness. She was *Englisch*, and this wonderful family was Amish. Everyone knew that the Plain and the fancy did not mix, not even when a compassionate man and two adorable children made an *Englischer* feel like part of their family. If only things could be different, but Lily had to accept life as it was. She was not Amish. She was Violet Hudson's daughter, and she needed to return to her taxi business at the foot of the mountain, even if leaving this sweet family would make her so very sad.

FOURTEEN

Lily did the dishes while Fannie went upstairs to gather more items for sale. Not long after Matthias left to take the children to school, a car turned into the drive. Lily hurried to the window to see who had arrived, worried that it could be Peterson. She didn't know whether to be relieved or concerned when she saw the sheriff.

"Is something wrong?" she asked when she opened the door.

"After our conversation, I knew we needed to talk." He glanced down nervously. "Do you mind if I come in?"

She stepped back and motioned him inside, but she'd didn't invite him to the table or offer him a cup of coffee. She wanted to keep the meeting short. Although he had to notice the Amish dress she wore, he didn't mention her attire.

"Look, we've got some bad water under

bridge in our relationship, Lily, and I felt we needed to talk in person."

She pursed her lips. "Our relationship wasn't the problem. Your relationship with my mother was."

He shrugged. "I know you think I was using Violet, but I loved her."

"Humph." Lily wrapped her arms around her waist. "Do you think I'm as gullible as my mother and will believe your lies?"

"I didn't come here to change your mind, but the truth is your mother swept me off my feet. I wasn't thinking of my son, or my position here in the community or the wife I had married in my youth and had pledged to stay with until death."

"No, you were only thinking of your own happiness."

"I was thinking of your mother, too, and how much I wanted to be with her."

Lily sighed. *Once a liar, always a liar.*

"I can't make it up to you or to her. I was thinking with my heart instead of my head. My son's school work took a turn for the worse about that time, and I knew I had to start being a father and the leader of my family." He glanced away and swallowed. "That meant saying goodbye to Violet."

"Convenient that everything happened when

the rumors were flying that she was involved in Noelle's death."

"Your mother never would have hurt Noelle. She couldn't hurt anyone. I tried to stop the rumors when they surfaced. Noelle's death had nothing to do with me splitting up with your mother. The fact was, you both needed to leave Sunview before some overzealous townsperson decided to take matters into his or her own hands. I knew I couldn't adequately protect either of you when you were living in the country some distance from town. You had to leave for your own safety, although I don't think your mother would have left if it hadn't been for you. She didn't want anything to happen to you."

Lily didn't believe him. "How easy it is to make up a story now."

He shook his head. "It's the truth, whether you believe me or not. If your mother hadn't left Sunview, I might have asked her to take me back. With her out of town, I was forced to try to correct the mistakes I had made with my family."

"Which appears to have worked out for you."

"Except Roxanne never lets me forget what happened."

Lily stared into his trouble eyes and recognized pain there. If the sheriff was telling the truth, he, too, had carried a heavy load all these years.

"Did you ever try to contact my mother?"

He glanced down. "I found out where you lived in Macon and drove there one night. You were waitressing at a local diner."

Lily nodded. "The Lazy Loon. I worked the five-to-eleven shift."

"I asked your mother's forgiveness and tried to convince her that we could make a go of it, but she wouldn't hear of it. She said she had almost lost you when you both left Sunview. She refused to do anything to hurt you again."

Tears burned Lily's eyes. She had never realized her mother cared about her feelings.

The sheriff looked embarrassed, no doubt because of the depth of emotion he had shared. Then he straightened his shoulders. "As I mentioned on the phone, I'll be at the lodge this afternoon. If you're there, I'd appreciate your help."

"What do you want me to do?"

"Be vigilant, and scout out the guests at the festival. If you see Peterson, let me know."

The sheriff gave her his cell phone number.

"I'll help you on one condition," Lily said.

"What's that?"

"That you stop the rumors about my mother and reopen the investigation. Noelle's death needs to be solved."

"I've tried, Lily."

"Then try a little harder."

Fannie came down the stairs. She stared at the sheriff and scowled. "I heard talking, but I did not expect to see the sheriff in my kitchen. Is something wrong?"

Lily explained about the sheriff's request for her help.

"I'll be escorting Clay Lambert to the lodge this afternoon," he added. "I'll remain until the festivities are over and the crowds have gone home or back to their rooms at the lodge."

"And what of Lily?" Fannie pressed.

"I'll make sure one of my deputies stays near her at all times."

"I trust you are a man of your word?" Fannie stared at the sheriff.

He shuffled his feet before nodding. "Yes, ma'am. My word is my bond."

"This is *gut* to know." Fannie pointed to the stove. "The coffee is hot. You would like a cup before you head back to town?"

"I'll take a rain check." He turned to Lily. "You have my number. Don't hesitate to call."

After the sheriff left the house, Fannie poured two cups of coffee and motioned Lily toward the table. She accepted the hot brew from Fannie's hand and settled into one of the chairs. Fannie sat across from her and sipped from her cup.

Finally, she said, "I could not help but overhear some of the sheriff's conversation. He has a big voice, *yah*?"

"My mother didn't always make the best decisions."

"We all make mistakes."

Lily smiled ruefully. "I doubt you do, Fannie."

The older woman snorted. "I judged the sheriff without knowing the facts." She patted Lily hand. "Back then, I knew he had a woman and had been unfaithful, but I did not know who the woman was." She paused for a long moment. "He bared his soul to you, Lily. He loved your mother, but he wanted to be true to his marriage vows. This is a wise decision of a man who realized his mistake. Unfortunately, your mother was hurt and suffered." She stared into Lily's eyes. "You suffered as well."

"My relationship with my mother was never good, and it soured even more when Noelle died. I blamed my mother for forcing me to leave high school and Sunview before graduation."

"And you still carry that pain."

Once again, tears burned Lily's eyes. "I can't forgive her, much as I want to."

"You think forgiveness comes from the heart, but it comes from the head." She tapped her finger against her brow. "You make the decision to forgive even if it is difficult and you do not feel that forgiveness. The mistake made might always bring pain, but you do not wish condemnation on the person who hurt you."

"I... I don't understand."

"Too often people think forgiveness means accepting the other person back into your life and being able to ignore what happened. When the wound is deep and there is much pain, this does not make sense, and, thus, you are never able to forgive."

"So what's the answer?"

"Just as I said. You forgive with your intellect. The mistake still hurts. You still regret having to leave town, but you go on, and you don't dwell on your mother's mistake. Nor do you bring it up to her time and again. You wipe the slate clean, as a teacher would say. You still remember, and perhaps you even remain cautious and guarded around the person who hurt you."

"You mean if I proclaim it with my lips, then I have forgiven her?"

"Maybe, but you need to keep working to move past the pain."

Fannie took another sip from her cup. "Right now, you are allowing the mistake and the pain to be like an open wound. You did not return to Sunview because of it. You did not want to reconnect with any of the friends you had in high school. You did not want to be seen in town, and chances are, you wanted nothing to do with your mother. You closed her out of your life just as you closed yourself to Sunview."

The woman sighed. "You and Matthias are a lot alike. He has closed his heart to finding love again because of what happened to Rachel. He blames himself."

Lily waited for Fannie to continue.

"You have closed not only your heart, Lily, but also your life. You want to live in a sheltered world where nothing painful can hurt you again."

"I don't think that's it."

"Are you not planning to leave Sunview?"

Lily nodded. "I am, but only because Matthias must go on with *his* life, and I am too much of a distraction."

Fannie smiled and nodded. "This is true, but as I mentioned earlier, you are making him realize he should not be alone."

"Yet I am *Englisch*."

"That is the problem."

"So what do I do, Fannie?"

"First, you must get rid of bitterness and anger. Only then can you see the future through a clear lens."

"I… I don't understand."

Fannie patted her hand and then stood. "Then I will pray that you find your way and decide what is right for your future."

The kitchen door opened and Matthias stepped inside. Along with him came a blast of cool air. He looked as confused as Lily felt. "I saw the sheriff's patrol car pass the schoolhouse. Is there a problem?"

Fannie took her cup to the sink. "Lily will tell you. I need to check the hen house for eggs."

She walked outside, leaving Lily even more confused. She would tell Matthias about the sheriff asking for her help, but she wouldn't tell Matthias about not being able to forgive her mother. Most especially, Lily wouldn't tell him about her inability to forgive herself for what had happened the night Noelle had been walking near the snowy country road. She had never told anyone. Her mother knew. That was part of the problem in their relationship, and even though her mother never talked about what had happened, it remained a wedge between them.

Lily couldn't forgive her mother for falling in love with the sheriff, and she couldn't forgive herself for her own hardness of heart. She had thought only of herself that night. She hadn't thought of Noelle and her need because she hadn't been able to forgive Noelle and her perfect family for accusing her mother of being a thief. That had started the terrible spiral that forced Lily and her mother to leave town.

The Amish had a strong faith, and Lily pretended she had a relationship with the Lord, but it was a lie, because *Gott*, as Matthias would say, wouldn't have anything to do with someone who had made so many mistakes in her life.

How could she expect Matthias to be interested in her when her whole life was a mistake? She would leave Sunview tomorrow, but today she would attempt to find Peterson so the hateful man could be brought to justice. Sheriff Granger had indicated that he would stop the rumors about her mother. That in itself would make her trip to Sunview a success, except—

She sighed.

Her feelings for Matthias would remain. Just like her mother, she would leave a man who had taken up residence in her heart. She would never forget Matthias, and she doubted she would ever be able to find a man equally as good, but she couldn't stay here in Sunview.

One night. She had to endure one more night before she said goodbye to Matthias and his children and his Amish life. Saying goodbye to him would be the hardest thing she'd ever have to do.

Not long after Matthias returned home from delivering his children to school, he and Lily climbed into the buggy and took the back roads that led to the entrance of the lodge. Matthias kept his gaze on not only the road, but also the area around them. Peterson was on the loose, and after his repeated attacks on Lily, Matthias needed to remain vigilant.

Lily looked lovely in the Amish clothing, and he felt sure anyone would have a difficult time identifying her as the woman who had stumbled into his life just a few days earlier. Perhaps it was the fresh December air, but her complexion had taken on a healthy sheen, and although she was somewhat subdued, her determination to not let Peterson get the upper hand seemed stronger than ever.

Matthias parked in an area reserved for buggies and helped Lily down. "Keep watch, and let me know if you see anyone who looks like Peterson. Remember he could have altered his looks just as you have."

She glanced quickly around. "What will the other Amish people say? Will they recognize me as not being authentic?"

"If anyone asks, tell them you are getting to know the Amish ways. I have no doubt that you'll find them to be accepting and welcoming."

"Fannie taught me a few more Pennsylvania Dutch words, but nothing that will help me carry on a conversation."

"Again, explain that you're learning the dialect. It is necessary before baptism, so you will be considered as someone seeking entry into the church community. They will embrace you. Plus, I will remain close in case anyone seems too interested in who you really are."

"Thank you, Matthias."

He took her hand. "Do not worry about the Amish, Lily. Your only concern should be Peterson."

She nodded, and his heart went out to her. She was vulnerable, yet he knew she had an underlying strength and was committed to not let anything, including Peterson, ruin her life.

After the festival, she would return to her previous way of life, and he would return to his. Truth be told, he would miss her, miss her smile, her beautiful eyes and the softness of her skin, her enthusiasm and the way she uplifted his children.

She uplifted him as well.

Turning, she caught his gaze. "You look pensive, Matthias."

He shook out of his thoughts. "Sorry, I was thinking of after you leave. The children will miss you."

She continued to stare at him, and he wanted to tell her that he would miss her, too, but he had already said and done too much. Recalling their kiss last night, he knew he had stepped over the line.

People were flooding into the grounds. He waved at a number of Amish families he knew as they headed to the booth. He was grateful that everyone was focused on their work and did not notice the woman walking next to him dressed in Amish clothing. But Matthias noticed her. He could think of little else except the beautiful woman who seemed to have taken residence in his heart.

FIFTEEN

Lily was on edge as she and Matthias opened the booth and began to arrange the wares. She kept flicking her gaze at the other vendors' stalls and the people who meandered around the periphery of the lodge. Her neck was tense, and she rubbed her shoulders to ease the stress while she arranged the items on the shelving. Matthias had brought a binder with sketches of the furniture he made. Hopefully, that would attract buyers, too.

A few Amish people waved and said hello as they passed by. Everyone seemed focused on preparing for the festival that would start later that day.

Mr. and Mrs. Keeper came out of the lodge and circulated through the various stands. Both of them had always been nice to Lily and warm and hospitable when she spent time with Noelle. Mrs. Keeper had often made hot chocolate and baked cookies as an afternoon snack.

The memory of those times surrounded by the pretty furnishings in the Keepers' suite and the fine china and sterling flatware at their table had made an impression on Lily. She hadn't coveted their material possessions, however, she had longed for a stable life and a peaceful home filled with love.

Noelle's murder had been a shock and had unsettled Lily and her mother so much. Leaving Sunview had been their only option, especially when people claimed Lily's mother could be an accomplice in Noelle's death.

Mrs. Keeper walked by Matthias's stall, then she glanced back and stared at Lily. Lowering her gaze, Lily's heart pounded. What would she say if Mrs. Keeper realized the Amish woman with Matthias was really Noelle's playmate from the past?

"Matthias, you'll be taking our guests for buggy rides later today?" Mrs. Keeper asked.

He smiled. "*Yah*, I'll start giving rides at four o'clock, if that sounds *gut* to you."

Mrs. Keeper nodded. "The parade in town will be over, and our special singer will be heading to the lodge. Soon after that, the guests will enjoy dinner and prepare for the entertainment."

"It should be a lovely evening," Matthias said.

Mrs. Keeper smiled at Lily. Unwilling to return the gesture, Lily bowed her head even lower and pretended to focus her attention on the wreaths she had made.

The lodge owner stared at her for a long moment. "You look familiar. Have we met?"

Matthias stepped forward. "My mother will be here later with the children. She said to give you a loaf of her cranberry walnut bread to enjoy with your coffee, *yah*?"

He handed her the wrapped loaf.

Mrs. Keeper beamed with pleasure. "Be sure to thank Fannie for me, Matthias. I'll try to stop by after she arrives, but as busy as things become later in the day, I might not be able to thank her myself."

"I will ensure she knows of your gratitude." He picked up a wreath. "And accept this wreath as a small token of our appreciation for all you do for the people of Sunview."

The older woman's smile widened. "Again, thank you. I'll hang it on the back door."

As she hurried away, Lily let out a sigh of relief. "I was sure she'd recognized me."

"Perhaps something triggered her memory, yet with the Amish dress and *kapp*, she would not think of her teenage daughter's friend." He squeezed Lily's hand. "You can relax."

"I'm afraid that's impossible, especially if Peterson makes an appearance."

By early afternoon, the grounds were filled

with not only folks staying at the lodge, but also shoppers from the surrounding area. Lily was pleased with the number of sales and the interest in her merchandise as well as Matthias's furniture, yet she remained ever vigilant, knowing Peterson could be hiding in the crowd.

"This is better than any of the fairs around Pinewood," she told Matthias as she scanned the shoppers, searching for a camo jacket and a man with a limp.

Matthias was equally as vigilant and kept his focus on the crowd. "People come from as far away as Atlanta, Chattanooga and Knoxville. The Keepers have built this up into a well-advertised event. Having Clay Lambert as tonight's entertainment adds to the attraction."

He glanced at the clock hanging on the side of the porch. "The parade in town should be over by now, and some of the special guests will be heading this way soon."

Lily spied Fannie near the entrance. "Your mother and children have arrived."

Sarah and Toby ran to greet Lily, followed by Duke, who nuzzled Lily's leg. She patted the sweet dog and smiled at the children.

"Did you see the parade?" she asked as they hugged their father and then gave her a hug that warmed her heart.

"*Yah*, it was *wunderbar*."

Matthias left to help his mother with the horses while the children told Lily all they had seen. "A band played, and people rode in cars. Others were on horseback, and some of the businesses built floats and tossed candy to the children who lined the street."

"Did you get some candy?" she asked.

They nodded, their eyes wide. "*Mammi* let us have a chocolate bar and a peppermint. She put the other candy in her handbag and said we can have a piece later."

Fannie appeared carrying a box with more baked items. "Matthias said your merchandise is drawing customers to our stand, Lily."

"I'm sure your baked items and his woodworking are the draw, Fannie." She took the box from the older woman and arranged the freshly baked items on the shelves.

Fannie glanced around. "It is a large crowd, *yah*?"

Sarah pulled on her grandmother's hand. "The children are gathering near the stage to sing carols."

"Then you and Toby must join them."

Matthias returned to the stall with more merchandise. He placed the boxes in the booth and then grabbed the children's hands. "I'll walk you there."

The twins waved goodbye and scurried off

with their father to join the other children. Duke followed at their heels.

"It is a *gut* day, *yah*?" Fannie stated. Her smile faded. "Have you seen this Peterson man anywhere?"

Lily shook her head. "No sign of him."

"And the sheriff?"

"No sign of him, either."

Fannie *harrumphed*. "He talks out of both sides of his mouth, *yah*?"

Lily thought of the lies he had told her mother. "You're probably right, Fannie. He promises much but does not follow through with what he promises. My mother was proof of that."

Fannie grabbed her hand. "You are not your mother, and you do not have to apologize for her actions. She is her own person, and you are as well."

Lily appreciated Fannie's encouragement. "Yet my life was complicated by the choices she made."

"Of course, this is so, but remember those were your mother's decisions."

"Her health has declined, and her cognitive awareness is not as it should be, but my aunt takes good care of her, which allows me to work and not worry about her being alone."

"Does she know you're in Sunview?"

"I told her, but she gets confused. I want Peterson apprehended before I leave, but even if he's not, I have to go back to work and eventually find a new place to live."

Fannie glanced at the stall. "Yet you are working here." There was a glimmer in her eyes.

"And it looks like a profitable day, for sure, but I… I can't take advantage of your hospitality."

"Ack!" Fannie waved her hand. "There is no advantage taken. We have enjoyed your company, and the children are thrilled to have a young woman in the house again."

"They're precious children."

"They need a mother," Fannie said.

"Someday Matthias will find another woman to love."

Fannie pursed her lips. "Love is not always easy to find."

"But I'm sure many Amish women would enjoy Matthias's company."

Fannie nodded. "The widow Hershberger plies him with cakes and pies. Others do as well, but the problem is not with the women."

"You mean Matthias isn't interested in courting?"

"That is exactly what I mean. You have awakened something in him, dear, and this has been *gut* to see."

"Yet, I'm an *Englischer.*"

Fannie nodded. "But perhaps now, he will realize that it is time to look for love again."

Lily knew Fannie was right, but the idea of Matthias courting an Amish woman made her sad. She tried to shake off the feeling, yet the more she thought of Matthias with someone else, the gloomier she became.

On his way back to the booth, she saw him stop to talk to another Amish man. A woman stood nearby, smiling with interest at Matthias. She was pretty and young and totally Amish.

What was Lily trying to do by homing in on Matthias and his family? Tomorrow, she would leave Sunview and return to Pinewood and her taxi business. Hard as it would be to say goodbye, she had to leave now before her feelings for Matthias grew even stronger.

Promptly at four o'clock, Matthias steered his mare toward the rear of the lodge and the kiosk where eager children were waiting with their parents for a buggy ride. A number of other buggies were lined up to ferry the families around the extensive grounds. He glanced back to his own stall, where Lily and his mother were conversing with various shoppers interested in the items for sale.

Lily was a natural salesperson. Her sweet and friendly manner were both welcoming and charming. Shoppers felt at ease examining the items for sale without feeling pressure to purchase any of the merchandise. His mother's baked goods were always in demand, but Lily's crafts, wreaths and assortment of handmade Christmas ornaments and wall hangings were an even bigger draw.

In a gazebo closer to the water, he saw Sarah and Toby surrounded by other Amish children. The harmony of their sweet voices traveled over the grounds and warmed his heart as they sang old favorite Christmas hymns a cappella. The children attracted a crowd of onlookers who seemed enchanted by the musical performance. So far, Peterson hadn't caused a problem. Once again, Matthias scanned the crowd for anyone who seemed to fit his description.

Matthias's first riders were a mom and dad and two young children who were wide-eyed as he pulled the mare to a stop in front of the kiosk. Matthias helped them into the buggy and chatted about the history of the lodge and the community of Sunview, where the Amish and *Englisch* lived in peaceful harmony.

The ride lasted a quarter of an hour and allowed Matthias to search a greater swath of guests. Relieved though he was that no one fit Peterson's description, he remained on edge. The children were rosy-cheeked when he returned them to the starting point. Matthias and the other Amish men continued to provide rides for the next hour.

"Part of the parade from town is arriving soon," one of the staff members from the lodge announced. "Line the entrance drive as Clay Lambert and his entourage appear and give him a warm North Georgia welcome."

Matthias tethered his mare and headed back to the booth. His mother was placing more baked breads and pies on the shelves. He glanced around, looking for Lily.

"I told her to join the people at the front gate so she could see Clay when he arrives." Fannie pointed to an Amish family standing close to the drive. "The children went with the Troyers. They were eager to see the parade, and I didn't think you would mind."

"Of course not. The Troyers are a lovely family." He glanced at the gate in the distance, hoping to see Lily.

His mother made a shooing motion. "Go and find her. She will enjoy your company."

"You're all right here at the stall?"

"I am fine. With everyone focused on the entertainment, I'll have an opportunity to catch my breath." Again, she motioned him away. "Hurry or you will miss the main star. From what people say, he has a strong voice and should provide an excellent concert this evening."

"I won't be gone long," he promised before he hurried to join the people amassing near the entrance gate.

The jovial atmosphere was heartwarming. Just as in years past, the Keepers had brought together an amazing assortment of entertainment and vendors to make the festival a success.

Matthias searched for Lily, but by wearing a blue dress and *kapp*, she fit in with the many Amish women, which left Matthias confused as to where she could be. Well-meaning people shoved in around him. Standing taller than many of those gathered, he continued to scan the crowd and grew more concerned when he failed to see Lily.

The first car in the caravan crested the rise heading through the entrance to the grounds of the lodge. A man drove the lead convertible, and even from a distance, Matthias recognized Clay's mother in the passenger seat. Just as at the comfort station, she wore a red jacket with the logo of the Christmas Lodge on the breast pocket. She was well-liked by the vendors and was always eager to help if anyone had problems in their setup or during the festival.

Her son, Clay, sat on the back of the rear seat. He was dressed in a thick wool coat with a red scarf around his neck. He wore his hair long around his ears and had a well-trimmed beard. From the shouts and applause of the crowd, he was a sure favorite.

A few more cars followed, including the mayor of Sunview with his wife and a handful of other notable guests. The sheriff's car, with lights flashing, was the last vehicle in the caravan. The security force at the lodge was made up of local men who had little experience with hard-core criminals, so having the sheriff and his deputies onsite filled Matthias with relief.

He spied an Amish woman who looked like Lily on the opposite side of the road. She had her back to him, so he couldn't be certain.

"Excuse me." He tried to weave his way around the people gathered near him. Everyone was in an exuberant mood. They chatted eagerly among themselves and continued to bunch up around him.

He glanced across the entrance drive to where he had seen the woman just moments earlier and groaned. She was gone. Had it been Lily?

He tried to calm his frustration. Lily had to be nearby, yet the more he searched for her, the more worried he became. Much as he hated to admit it, Lily had gone missing.

SIXTEEN

Lily would have recognized Clay Lambert anywhere. He had a wide smile and gave a friendly wave as he passed by the enthusiastic crowd. If anyone could wear their fame well, it was Clay. He seemed, at least from what she could tell, as down-to-earth and accessible as he had been in his youth.

Betsy appeared in the distance with a clipboard in hand. She talked to a woman on staff and then hurriedly returned to the lodge.

Glancing back at Matthias's booth, Lily's heart sank when she didn't see him. She had hoped he would take a break from the buggy rides, and although she scanned the area, she couldn't find him in the crowd. Where could he be?

All around her were Amish and *Englisch* families enjoying the festival together. Instead of feeling self-conscious in the Amish clothing, she felt like she fit in. She doubted anyone would recognize her, whether she ran into a friend from high school or even Peterson.

Just thinking of him made her shiver. She wrapped her arms around her waist and turned to gaze at the lodge. The wreath Matthias had given Mrs. Keeper hung on the rear door and brought to mind memories of her youth. She and Noelle would often play in the turret room and race up and down the narrow back stairway that led outside to the expansive grounds and rolling hills.

Saddened by recalling her once-upon-a-time friendship with Noelle, Lily turned back to the lead car. Kevin Granger was driving. He glanced at Lily and then flicked his gaze to the roadway. From his placid expression, she knew he hadn't recognized her. Mrs. Lambert sat in the passenger seat and waved to the crowd. Her smile was infectious, and from her exuberance, anyone could see that she was proud of her son. Mrs. Lambert had raised Clay to be a great guy who had worked hard to achieve fame with his singing.

Lily thought of her own mother, who had worked hard, too, yet she had been fired from the lodge when money had mysteriously disappeared from Mrs. Keeper's office.

Once again, Lily thought of the earlier happy times when she was a child. She saw an elderly man with gray hair and an equally gray beard shuffle along the wraparound porch. He was bent over and used a cane. Her heart went out to him, and she was concerned about his ability to navigate the stairs due to his frailty. She couldn't recall seeing him previously, nor did she recognize the dark wool coat and gray slacks he wore, yet for some reason, he seemed familiar.

She continued to watch as he hooked his cane over his arm and climbed down the porch steps without difficulty.

At the foot of the steps, he scanned the crowd for a long moment. Then, as if drawn by a magnet, his gaze met hers.

Her heart stopped. The man was old and bent and dressed in clothing she didn't recognize, but for the briefest moment, she wondered if he was Pete Peterson.

Matthias fought through the crowded area, still trying to find Lily. After making sure his children were still with the Troyer family, he turned his focus back to the crowd.

Out of the corner of his eye, he saw a flash of blue and realized Lily was running toward the parking lot on the far side of the lodge. Her hair was spilling from her bun, and her *kapp* flying in the air.

His heart pounded. He broke into a fast sprint and headed after her.

"Lily," he called, but the crowd cheering for Clay Lambert drowned out his voice. She kept running.

"Lily," he called again.

She turned and spied him, then she pointed to the parking lot. A number of cars were leaving the area and heading back to town. Probably people who did not plan to stay for the evening performance.

He caught up to her and grabbed her arm. "What happened?"

"An old man. I didn't recognize him at first, but then he turned and caught my gaze."

"Peterson?"

She nodded. "I think so. He walked with a cane. He was wearing a wool coat and had gray hair and a gray beard. He ran toward the parking lot."

"Are you sure it was him?"

She stared at the string of cars and shrugged as she turned again to Matthias. "I'm not sure of anything. Maybe I was imagining it was him."

The sheriff hurried toward them. "I saw you both running and thought something had happened."

Lily filled him in on what she had seen.

"I'll ask at the lodge and see if anyone recognizes the old man's description. Plus, I'll alert lodge security as well as my deputies. Tonight's the high point of the festival. We don't need anyone causing trouble."

She bristled. "I'm not causing problems."

The sheriff exhaled. "I wasn't referring to you. I'm talking about Peterson."

Matthias interrupted. "Lily needs to go back to my house with my mother and children. I'll stay here to man the booth."

The sheriff raised his hand. "I need her here. She's the only one who can recognize Peterson."

"I'm staying." Lily turned to Matthias. "But you're right that your mother and children should go home. They'll miss the show, yet they need to be safe."

"You need to be safe as well," Matthias insisted.

"I told you," the sheriff said, seemingly vexed. "She's needed here. My deputies and I will make certain no harm comes to her."

Matthias pursed his lips. "You haven't helped her before this, Sheriff. I'm not sure why you think you can help now."

Granger let out a frustrated breath. "If anything happens, I'll have one of my deputies take Lily home. Plus, I'll get one of my men to drive your mother and children to your farm. He can ensure they're securely inside your house before he returns to the lodge."

The sheriff looked at where Clay, his mother and a few of the other people in his entourage were leaving their cars and heading into the lodge. "I've got to talk to Clay's manager. Give me a few minutes, and my deputy will meet your family near the front gate."

Once the sheriff headed back to the lodge, Matthias and Lily joined Fannie at the booth. The children were there eating corn dogs.

"Night will fall soon," Matthias told the children. "It's time for you to go home with *Mammi*."

"Do we have to go?" they asked.

"*Yah*, your *datt* is right," his mother agreed. "On the way, we will have some of the candy you got at the parade."

The children clapped their hands.

"Plus, there's a surprise." He told them about the deputy taking them home.

"What about our buggy?" Fannie asked.

"I'll ask the oldest Troyer boy to drive it home for us later."

"We are going for a ride in a police car?" Toby eyes were wide.

"In the sheriff deputy's car," Matthias corrected. "The deputy can explain how his radio works, and maybe he'll flash his lights."

The children were excited. As they hugged

Lily, Fannie leaned close to Matthias so the children couldn't hear. "Be careful tonight. If Peterson is around, both you and Lily could be in danger."

"I'm not worried about myself."

"No, but you are worried about her. She should come home with us."

"The sheriff needs her here to identify Peterson in case he shows up again."

"And what if he attacks you on the way home."

"I trust one of the deputies will escort us as well, *Mamm*. Do not worry."

Fannie raised her brow. "You're a parent, Matthias. Do you not worry about leaving your children?"

What his mother said was true. He did worry about what would happen to his children if anything happened to him, and he should have worried more about Rachel. Why hadn't he realized she was having trouble and needed medical help?

He glanced at Lily, who was talking with the children. He couldn't let something happen to another woman who had taken hold of his heart. He needed to ensure Lily remained safe.

Matthias and Lily walked his mother and children to the entrance drive where the deputy was waiting for them. As Fannie and the children climbed into his vehicle, Matthias waved goodbye and offered a silent prayer. *Protect my family, dear Gott.* He glanced at Lily. *Keep this woman who has stolen a part of my heart safe as well.*

SEVENTEEN

Lily was relieved when the children and Fannie were secure in the sheriff deputy's car and driving away from the lodge. The children were excited about their special transportation and seemed happy with the candy Fannie had given them.

"It is better that they go home and are not here," Matthias said as he waved goodbye.

"I thought they would be disappointed to miss the performance."

He laughed. "A ride in the deputy's car tops listening to a singer they don't know."

"I guess you're right." She glanced at the crowd that had moved away from the entrance. Some folks were heading for the lodge, others were strolling around the grounds.

"We had better return to the booth." He placed his hand on the small of her back and ushered her along a wooded path that led to the vendor area.

"Thank you for your help, Lily. Your crafts have attracted much more interest to our stall. I've taken a number of orders for furniture and baby cradles."

"Your work is excellent, Matthias. I have a feeling word will spread."

"We Amish believe word of mouth is the best marketing strategy. A happy customer tells his or her friends, and business grows."

"Perhaps Toby will help you when he gets a bit older."

"He has his own small set of tools and often lends a hand."

"And Sarah?"

"She sands the wood for me. Her eye is *gut*, and she has a head for figures, so she can work the measurements."

"A family business."

Matthias's gaze narrowed. "A business that includes a father and his twin children. This is a broken family, Lily."

"Yet there is no doubt about the love that is between you."

He nodded. "Love between a father and his children is strong, yet there is another love that is needed as well."

Lily's heart pounded, and her throat went dry. What was Matthias saying?

"I'm sure there is a lovely Amish woman in your future."

He reached out his hand and touched her arm. "Sometimes we do not see what is before us."

She saw him, but she couldn't express her feelings. He was Amish, and she was not, even though she wore Amish clothing.

"Sometimes we are fooled into believing someone is good for us, but that may be a momentary feeling that will change with time." She glanced at the setting sun and the mountains in the distance. "Some hills are too hard to climb, Matthias."

"But even steep mountains can be scaled if one is determined."

"And what if the obstacles are too great?" she asked.

"A committed man keeps trying."

Lily glanced around again, searching for any sign of Peterson. The crowd had dissipated, and most of the people had moved toward the front of the lodge. She and Matthias were surrounded by a thick stand of trees. The setting sun cast them in shadow.

He leaned closer, and her heart pounded even more rapidly.

She could smell his clean scent, and she saw the depth of his feelings written all too plainly on his face and in the recesses of his eyes.

She stared at him and lost herself in his gaze. She didn't care about what divided them—she thought only of Matthias and the way she felt complete and whole when she was around him, something she had never felt before. She wasn't a high school girl who no one wanted to befriend or a young woman who had to work hard to make ends meet and didn't know what her future would hold. With Matthias, she wanted a future with him.

He rubbed her arm, and for a split second she forgot about the danger that surrounded them.

"Matthias?" a man's voice.

He pulled back.

She blinked, suddenly embarrassed by the Amish man who was staring at them.

"Someone wants to place an order for outdoor furniture. I told them I would find you."

Matthias nodded. "Thank you, Amos. I'll go to the stall now."

Again, he placed his hand on the back of Lily's waist and searched the crowd as he guided her into the vendors' area where the people milled around.

Her world had crashed to a standstill the moment the man had interrupted them. Her cheeks burned. What had she done? She and Matthias could never be together.

Lily was so her mother's daughter. She had

given her heart to a man who was off-limits. Just as her mother had done. Lily had to leave town and leave Matthias and his family no matter how much she wanted to stay.

Her heart was heavy. She hadn't wanted to leave Sunview when she was a teen. She didn't want to leave tomorrow. Most of all, she didn't want to leave Matthias.

Matthias was encouraged by the large order the customer placed, but his heart was thoroughly confused by the close moment he had shared with Lily, and he remained ever worried about her safety. He'd never felt such a mix of emotion as well as concern. Plus, he had overstepped his bounds. The *Ordnung* was specific about Amish marrying an *Englischer*. It was *vorgeriddelt*. Forbidden, yet he couldn't imagine anything was wrong when he felt such a connection with Lily.

The heavy weight on his shoulders that he'd carried since losing Rachel had lifted, and he saw the world in a new light. The future had promise instead of being an endless line of days that offered little joy, other than the joy of being with his children. He had been right when he told Lily that a man needed a different kind of love. He needed a woman to walk with him. It was the way *Gott* had created the world from the very beginning.

Yet, when he glanced at Lily as she chatted with a woman interested in some of her tree ornaments, he wondered if he was fooling himself into thinking something could come of their relationship.

Could he leave his faith? Not when he had children to raise. He wanted them to grow up knowing the sense of family and community, to have a strong love for *Gott* and a good moral compass. Yes, that could happen in the *Englisch* world, but it would be more difficult there, and he had a responsibility to raise his children in the faith. It's what he and Rachel had planned to do, and even though his heart had opened to Lily, he could not cause distress to his children.

He glanced at Lily again. She looked beautiful and so comfortable in the long dress and *kapp*. If only she had given him some clue that she might be interested in joining his faith.

Turning away, he sighed as he glanced at the various shoppers. How could a woman who drove a taxi and who was not deterred by a man who was trying to kill her, how could a strong, determined woman like that be happy in the Amish life?

The bishop would tell Matthias that he was dreaming like a foolish youth on *rumspringa*, but he didn't feel like a kid—he felt like a man who knew what he wanted.

When the customer stepped away with her purchase, Matthias moved closer to Lily, wanting to keep her safe and wishing he could tell her how he felt tonight. He glanced up, seeing the full moon over the lake. The twinkling lights and the sound of carolers as they strolled around the grounds. This evening should have been so special, but a killer was on the loose and no matter how charming the surroundings were, Lily remained in danger.

She nudged his arm. "You have another customer."

He turned to see a man and woman approaching the stall. "We heard you make the best patio furniture."

"I do not make the best, but I make the best I can make, and the furniture is for both inside or outside, for a covered patio or an open deck." He pointed to the sketches of his work. "Let's talk about what you had in mind."

The twill of a cell phone interrupted his conversation. He turned to see Lily raise her cell to her ear. She mumbled something and then disconnected.

"It was the sheriff," she whispered so only he could hear.

Matthias's heart pounded.

"He wants me to meet him at the far side of the lodge."

"I'll tell the customers to come back later."

She grabbed his arm. "No, Matthias, take their order. I'll be fine."

But as she hurried away, he knew he had made a mistake in letting her go. He turned to the people watching him with confused expressions. "Could you excuse me for a few minutes? I'm needed on the other side of the lodge, but I'll return shortly."

"Of course, that won't be a problem."

He hurried after Lily, but just that fast, he had lost her in the crowd. He ran to the far side of the lodge where a few families gathered round a firepit. A person strummed a guitar and led the folks in carols while children romped on the grassy knoll.

But Lily, where was Lily?

EIGHTEEN

Lily met up with the sheriff at the rear of the lodge and hurried after him to the parking lot.

"This time, I think we've found your guy," he told her.

"Peterson?" She had to walk quickly to keep up with Granger's long strides.

"One of my deputies has him detained."

If only that could be true, but when she neared the deputy's patrol car where the man was being questioned, her enthusiasm plummeted. Although he was wearing a camo jacket, the man wasn't Peterson.

She shook her head.

The sheriff's face fell. "You're sure?"

"I'm positive."

Lily hurried back to the lodge, but instead of heading to the vendor area where she had left Matthias, she climbed the steps to the expansive porch lined with rows of rocking chairs. Children sat next to their parents, enjoying the mild night and the beautiful sky. Maintenance teams were on the stage located at the edge of the lake. They were adjusting the lighting and the sound system as unobtrusively as they could. Fireworks would light the sky after the show, and the pyrotechnicians were doing a last minute check on their anchored platforms out on the water.

In spite of Peterson, Lily anticipated a wonderful show with Clay Lambert's singing and then an amazing finale with fireworks. The door to the lobby opened and a family hurried outside. Chairs had been set up on the lawn leading to the water's edge, and folks were starting to find their seats.

Entering the lobby made Lily pause. Her heart pounded as she looked around the grand sitting area. Many of the couches and overstuffed chairs were filled with family groups as well as folks who may have met here at the lodge. A coffee carafe and dessert cart sat to the side of the reception desk, and the concierge was pointing folks to their seats outside.

"The show will start in less than fifteen minutes," he announced as he motioned the guests toward the door. "Don't forget your map of the hotel and the lodge."

Lily recognized the cover of the brochure as the same one she had seen on the flash drive file Matthias had found in her car. She glanced up at the lobby's high ceiling and the large chandelier hanging over the round cherry table. A pile of brochures were neatly arranged on the hardwood table next to an elaborate poinsettia and holly arrangement that matched the decorations around the room as well as the numerous trees with twinkling white lights and large red bulbs.

Mrs. Keeper raced through the lobby, waving to a few friends, and then headed outside. Mr. Keeper followed behind his wife a bit more slowly. He looked older and more infirm, which made Lily's heart ache. Noelle's father had always been a nice man who treated her as he would anyone and not a young teen whose mother worked in housekeeping. She watched him trail his wife outside, knowing he wouldn't recognize her even if he glanced her way.

For some reason, folks didn't focus on the Amish. Instead, they seemed to lump them into a generalized group that didn't warrant their attention. Lily wanted to make certain she always looked at each person as an individual, seeing their innate goodness and beauty and their strengths instead of oversimplifying who they were or how they would react in any particular situation.

She stepped up to the large picture windows that looked out to the porch and expansive front lawn, where people were gathering to watch the performance. Turning over the brochure to the back cover, she studied the sketch of the various rooms on the ground floor and then the guest rooms on the additional floors, including the grand turret room at the top.

Retracing her steps to the front lawn, she looked back at the lodge standing in the fading evening light. The various rooms were lit and some of the guests had opened their windows as if preparing to watch the performance from the comfort of their suites.

Once more, Lily glanced at the brochure and then up at the rooms, then turned to view the stage before she faced the lodge again. Pulling out her phone, she accessed the files she had saved from Peterson's flash drive and opened the graphic that had accompanied the brochure. A map of sorts, perhaps?

Mrs. Keeper's voice sounded over the public address system. "Thank you to all our guests joining us for this year's Christmas festival performance. Take your seats or stand in the rear or spread a beach towel or blanket on the grass and get ready to welcome Clay Lambert to the Christmas Lodge."

Lily returned to the lobby and hurried to the front desk. The clerk was talking to an older woman who was requesting information about Sunview. Lily gazed over her shoulder at the outside stage.

The musicians had finished warming up and burst into a jaunty rendition of "We wish you a Merry Christmas." The crowd joined in the singing.

The older woman stepped away from the counter, and the clerk nodded to Lily. "How may I help you, ma'am?"

"Do you by any chance have a pencil and straight edge I could use for a few minutes?"

"Certainly." He rummaged in a drawer and handed her a ruler and mechanical pencil.

She moved to a nearby table, glanced at the graphic on her phone and then, using the ruler, drew a similar set of lines on the back of the brochure. Something was off, and she wasn't satisfied with what she had done. She reached for another brochure. This time she made an *x* in the middle of the paper before drawing the straight lines. For a long moment, she stared at the brochure with the lines superimposed and tried to determine what they meant. Slowly, an idea started to take hold.

Matthias's gut tightened. Night was falling, and although the lighting on the stage was bright, the floodlights around the lodge had been lowered to focus attention on the performance.

He flicked his gaze over the rolling grounds,

eyeing each group of people, hoping he could find Lily.

Where is she?

He raced to the front of the lodge. Mrs. Keeper stepped to the microphone on the stage as the last strains of "We Wish You a Merry Christmas" died down. A hush fell over the audience and their anticipation was palpable.

"It is an honor to welcome back to Christmas Lodge a talented singer whose rise to fame has been heartwarming and well-deserved." Mrs. Keeper's voice billowed over the enrapt crowd. "A local guy who came home to Sunview for Christmas and agreed to be with us tonight. Ladies and gentlemen, put your hands together in a warm Christmas Lodge welcome for Clay Lambert. As an added surprise, Clay promised to conclude his performance with my favorite, 'Home in Time for Christmas.'"

The crowd went wild with applause as Clay took the stage.

Matthias saw one of the deputies. He made his way through the crowd. "Have you seen Lily?"

"She was at the parking lot a few minutes ago. We were questioning a man who matched the appearance of her attacker, but she assured us we had the wrong guy."

"Where is she now?"

The deputy shrugged. "She may be with the sheriff." He pointed toward the opposite side of the stage. The sheriff was standing near the water so he could watch not only the performance but also the audience.

Matthias crossed the porch and climbed down the stairs that led to the vendor area. He hurried to his stall to ensure Lily hadn't returned.

Amos was standing between his own stall and the one Matthias manned. "Have you seen the woman who was helping me earlier?" he asked his friend.

"I have not seen her. Some folks had questions about your merchandise. I said you would be available after the performance."

"If Lily returns, ask her to stay here. Tell her I'll check back soon."

"*Yah*, I will tell her."

Nodding his thanks, Matthias hurried to where the sheriff was standing. The audience was clapping along with the singer as he sang a medley of Christmas favorites.

"Have you seen Lily?" He leaned close to the sheriff's ear in order to be heard.

"Isn't she at your booth?"

Matthias sighed. "I just checked there. Your deputy said he hasn't seen her since she left the parking lot."

"We thought the guy was Peterson. I've got

one of my men reviewing the lodge videos to ensure no one else with a beard and a limp is in the area. I also contacted law enforcement in Boulder Bluff."

"The town below Pinewood?"

The sheriff nodded. "I provided a description, long hair, beard and pronounced limp, and told them the date Peterson supposedly arrived in town."

"Did they know anything about him?"

"The description matches a man who stole a white sedan the night Lily drove him to Sunview."

"The car Lily saw in the ditch."

The sheriff nodded. "Roger that. Plus there was a cabin fire that they suspect a man named Bob Ingram may have started. Seems he and the guy we're calling Peterson are friends."

"Anyone in Boulder Bluff know why Peterson came to Sunview?"

"Nothing so far." He nodded toward the stage. "Although it has me worried. We've got a lot of high profile dignitaries in the audience." He pointed to a number of people in the first row, closest to the stage. "The mayor and his wife are here, along with a few state congressmen and one of our US senators. I want everything to run smoothly. We don't want any politicians to have a bad image of Sunview or the Christmas Lodge."

The sheriff's cell rang. He raised his mobile to his ear. "This is Sheriff Granger."

He nodded, then flicked his eyes over the crowd. "Negative, Walker. It looks good from my angle. Contact Sawyer and tell him to check the parking lot."

He disconnected and turned back to Matthias. "One of the videos showed a guy matching the description Lily provided. He was seen coming from the parking area carrying a long duffel bag."

"When?"

"A few minutes ago."

"What about Lily?"

"The deputy saw an Amish woman who could have been Lily near the comfort station."

Matthias turned to stare into the darkness. A small light in the distance revealed the comfort station where Lily had run into Peterson yesterday. Was he holed up in that area and, if so, did he have Lily?

"See if you can reach her on your cell."

The sheriff tried her number, then shook his head. "It disconnected and said the voice mail was full."

"I'll check the comfort station. We have to find Lily."

He turned to go, then glanced back at the sheriff. "We have to find her before it's too late!"

NINETEEN

Lily tried to call the sheriff, but he didn't answer his cell. She punched in Deputy Walker's number.

"This is Walker. How may I help you?"

"It's Lily. I couldn't reach the sheriff. I think Peterson is here."

"You've got that right. I spotted him on video. He was lurking around the north edge of the lodge."

"The side closest to the parking lot?"

"That's right. And he's carrying a long duffel bag."

"That duffel holds his rifle. He's here to do more than disrupt the event. He's being paid to do a job, and I'm guessing he plans to kill someone."

"The sheriff just got word that Peterson may be a former army sniper named Phil Philipson. He was court-martialed a few years back. His commanding officer believed he had killed one of the other soldiers in his unit, but it couldn't be proven, and the guy's death was labeled friendly fire."

"So now he's working as a hired gun, a sniper who's contracted to kill."

"If that's true, then things could go south quickly. The first row of guests, those sitting near the stage are VIPs, including state congressmen and a US senator."

Walker paused for a moment. "I've got another call coming in. We'll talk later." The deputy disconnected.

Lily glanced around the lobby. The elevator door was closing. Her heart stopped. For a split second, she had a glimpse of the person inside the elevator. He had long hair and a beard. Plus, he was carrying a duffel bag.

Pete Peterson was in the lodge.

She glanced down at the brochure and the graphic she had drawn. Her pulse picked up a notch. Near the stage where the dignitaries were sitting was the convergence point for all the lines in the graphic.

Her heart nearly stopped.

Peterson was here to kill one of the VIPs.

Matthias raced to the comfort station. He peered through the window, searching for any sign of Peterson or Lily, then pushed open the door and stepped into the darkened sitting area. Someone had turned off the overhead lighting.

He waited a moment until his eyes adjusted to the darkness and listened for any sound that could mean Lily was being held. He barely breathed, his body on high alert.

A small squeak came from the men's restroom.

He clutched the hefty stick he had found outside and inched his way toward the wash area. After pushing open the door, he waited. The automatic lights blinked on, and the sound of scurrying feet sounded. He peered down just as the mouse slithered out of sight.

He checked the various stalls, then announced his presence before he entered the women's area and checked those stalls.

Once he was certain no one was at the comfort station, he hurried back outside. The strains of the singer's voice carried over the property. He ran toward the lodge. He had wasted precious time on a wild-goose chase. Lily was in danger, and he feared she was in the killer's crosshairs.

TWENTY

As Lily climbed the stairs to the second floor, she tried to call the sheriff, but the connection failed. Once again, she checked the lines she had drawn on the brochure and put her ear to the door of the first room that intersected with a line on the graphic. Hearing nothing, she tried to turn the door knob and found it locked.

Before she could step away, an older woman opened the door. "I thought someone was at the door. May I help you?" she asked.

"I'm looking for a bearded man carrying a long duffel bag. Have you seen anyone matching that description?"

"No, dear, but I hope you can find your friend."

He wasn't Lily's friend.

She ran to the next room that had an expansive window with a view of the stage, a room that had been included in the graphic. Once again, she tried the door, then listened for sounds coming from within the room.

Hearing only silence, she glanced up and down the hallway, then tried the next door. Locked.

She gently knocked on the door. "Is anyone in there?"

A man stepped from the room across the hall. "Is there a problem?"

"Have you seen a bearded man with a limp carrying a long duffel bag?"

"A guy road the elevator up with me not long ago."

"Did he get off on this floor?"

The man shook his head. "He was still on when I exited."

Then Peterson was on the next floor. She raced up the stairs. Three rooms on that floor were connected to the graphic. She tried each of the doors but to no avail.

Her palms were wet, and her mouth ran dry.

She took the stairs to the next floor. The first door she approached opened. A man smiled, then looked confused. "Oh, sorry. I thought you were room service."

"No, sir." She peered into the room and saw a woman looking at the stage through the open window.

"Is Clay Lambert still performing?" Lily asked.

The man nodded. "His last song will be

'Home in Time for Christmas.' My wife's a big fan. But can I help you with something?"

Just as before, Lily asked if he had seen a man fitting Peterson's description.

"We've been in our room since after dinner."

The two additional rooms on that floor went unanswered.

Maybe she had been wrong. If Peterson wasn't holed up in one of the rooms, he could be on the lawn.

Again, she tried to call the sheriff. A computer-generated voice said he wasn't available. She tried Deputy Walker's number, but the connection failed.

If only she could determine where Peterson was? She thought of Matthias and knew he would be worried about her. She wanted to return to the booth and be with him, but she had to find Peterson. She knew how things could turn south in a flash, and she had a sinking feeling about tonight. Peterson was an army sniper, and he had brought his rifle to Sunview for something other than hunting wild game. He was hunting someone who he planned to kill. Then the job would be done, and he would collect the remainder of his payment.

She looked at her phone and clicked on the photo of the graphic. She compared it to the brochure and the map of the lodge where she had drawn the lines of convergence.

What wasn't she seeing?

She touched the screen and realized the top of the photo had been cut off on her phone. She shrunk the image to have a better view of the entire graphic.

Her pulse kicked up a notch. She hadn't noticed the longest line on the graphic. It stretched from the stage to the very top of the lodge—to the turret room where she and Noelle had played as children.

Peterson had to be there, but she needed to surprise him. The narrow back stairway she and Noelle had used when they played in the turret came to mind.

She raced down the stairs and hurried into the kitchen. A few of the workers were washing dishes and readying the breakfast supplies.

"Call security. Tell them to notify the sheriff. A killer's about to make a hit."

They looked confused.

"The sheriff," she repeated. "Call him."

She ran toward the small doorway near the pantry. Pulling in a shallow breath, Lily grabbed the doorknob and was relieved when the door opened. The stairway was even smaller than she remembered. She climbed the stairs, grateful the steps were carpeted to muffle the sounds of her footfalls. She passed the first floor, then the second. For a moment, she stopped to catch her breath. Her side ached and she wished she were in better shape.

Arriving at the third floor, she paused momentarily, then climbed the last flight of stairs. The air in the narrow stairway was stale, and she gasped.

Finally, she was at the very top. The door was ahead of her. What if it was locked?

She needed help. *Please, God. I haven't been faithful to Your precepts, but Fannie said You forgive, and that You want all Your children to turn to You in their need. I'm turning to You, and I need Your help.*

Clay Lambert's voice sounded in the stillness. "Home in time for Christmas is where I want to be," he crooned. His hit song and the last number in his performance.

Time was running out. If Peterson wasn't on the other side of that door, she would have failed. Then she would leave town once again in disgrace.

Pulling in a breath, she grabbed the knob and turned it ever so slowly. The door inched open. A cool breeze from the open window directly ahead fanned over her. In the distance, she could see the lights of the stage and the singer who stood high above the crowd, his arms outstretched as he sang the song that was a favorite. Her heart stopped. Peterson didn't plan to kill one of the VIPs, he planned to kill Clay Lambert.

A noise sounded, followed by a series of grunts. A bulky form stepped in front of the window. Beard, gray hair, camo jacket.

Peterson.

He raised a rifle to his shoulder and peered through the scope. He grunted again and hunkered down, readjusting the rifle on his shoulder. The singer hit the last note.

The crowd of onlookers cheered.

The sound reverberated in the turret room.

Peterson pulled in a breath.

Lily had to act now. Fearful though she was, she thought of the mistake she had made that night with Noelle. She couldn't make another mistake. She had to act. Fannie said mistakes often needed to be redeemed. Hopefully, the Lord would accept what she was about to do as redemption for her wrongdoing.

His finger drew back ever so slightly on the trigger.

Lily lunged out of her hiding spot and threw herself at him. The barrel of the rifle flew up. A shot sounded.

Peterson turned on her. "What are you doing?"

He kicked her and tried to realign his weapon.

She threw herself at him. Another round exploded. Her ears rang.

Growling, he raised the stock of the rifle and hit her in the stomach. The air *whooshed* from her lungs.

Once again, he kicked her, grabbed his duffel and raced out of the room.

Outside, people were screaming. The pretimed fireworks display exploded in the night sky, creating more chaos. She pulled herself up and peered through the window. Clay Lambert was lying on the stage. Lily hadn't stopped Peterson, and she hadn't saved Clay.

She had to keep Peterson from escaping.

Retracing her steps, she entered the narrow passageway. He would have to take the main stairwell, but if she hurried, she could get outside before him.

Gasping for air and trembling with fear, she clipped down the stairs. Instead of taking the exit into the kitchen, she headed to the door leading outside, where she and Noelle would run to play. The wreath she had made that Matthias had given Mrs. Keeper flew off the door as she opened it and dashed into the cool night.

The main stairwell door opened and Peterson raced outside. He saw her and raised his rifle. Again, she lunged at him.

"I should have killed you before." He shoved

her to the ground, lifted the rifle to his shoulder and aimed.

She rolled, trying to escape. He fired. The bullet nearly hit her. Dirt and gravel ricocheted around her, striking her face. She couldn't let him win.

"Please, God," she called out.

At that moment, a dog barked.

"What?" Peterson's eyes bulged.

Duke raced around the corner. He leaped just as Peterson turned to flee and landed on the guy's back, knocking him to the ground.

"Get him off me!" Peterson screamed.

Duke growled and nipped at Peterson's arm. The rifle lay at his side. Lily stumbled to her feet and grabbed the weapon.

Matthias rounded the corner of the lodge. " Lily, I couldn't find you."

"I had to stop Peterson," she said.

He took the rifle from her and handed it to the sheriff when he circled the building. Sirens sounded, and an ambulance pulled into the drive and stopped near them.

Two deputies helped Clay Lambert stagger toward the stretcher where EMTs treated his shoulder wound. His mother huddled nearby with Mr. and Mrs. Keeper, their faces ashen.

The sheriff handcuffed Peterson and pulled

him to his feet. "Keep the dog away from me," he said, cowering.

"What's your real name?" Granger asked.

Peterson remained silent.

"You're Phil Philipson, a former army sniper. You tried to kill someone in your unit and one of the K9s went after you."

"They didn't have any evidence. I wasn't found guilty."

"You were guilty of something to have a dishonorable discharge."

The sheriff read his Miranda rights.

"I want a lawyer," he cried.

Glancing at the sniper, Mrs. Keeper's face paled even more. She turned away from her husband and started walking toward the lodge.

"Where are you going?" Peterson yelled at her.

"Keep it down," the sheriff said.

"Ask her about hiring me."

The sheriff, Matthias and Lily all turned to stare at Mrs. Keeper.

Her husband looked confused and worried. "Honey, what's he saying?"

She raised her brow. "I told you, Roger, I needed closure concerning Noelle's death."

"But I thought we had closure after her funeral and burial."

"You might have, but I didn't." She shook

her head. "Not when her killer was still enjoying his fame."

"Don't tell me you hired this man." Mr. Keeper pointed to Peterson. "Did you hire him to kill Clay?"

"Why should he be alive when our Noelle is dead? It's been five years, or have you forgotten?"

Mr. Keeper's brow raised. "Why do you think Clay killed her?"

"I hired a private investigator, Roger. He found the autopsy report." Tears welled in her eyes. "Noelle was pregnant. She planned to meet Clay that night. They were going to run away together or at least that's what she thought. But he didn't want her with him. He wanted to go to Nashville alone for his record contract."

"Oh, honey," Mr. Keeper moaned. "You should have talked to me first."

"You would have stopped me, Roger. You were reconciled to her death."

"I wasn't reconciled, but I turned it over to God. I couldn't let the hate and anger eat at me any longer."

"But Clay *did* kill Noelle." She turned to the sheriff. "Arrest him. Arrest Clay Lambert for killing my daughter."

"Not so fast, ma'am," the sheriff said. "First,

I'll need to see what your private investigator dug up."

"Evidently, the autopsy report you claimed had nothing significant on it," Mr. Keeper said. "Why was that? Were you afraid your precious son Kevin was the father of Noelle's child?"

The look on the sheriff's face revealed that's exactly what he had thought.

"How could you think that, Dad?" Kevin stepped forward. "You may have hurt Mom, but I wouldn't do anything to hurt Noelle."

"Oh, son." The sheriff shook his head with remorse.

"I knew Noelle was secretly seeing someone else," Kevin continued, "but I didn't know it was my best friend."

He glared at Clay.

Tears glistened in the singer's eyes. "I loved Noelle. The PI was right. We were going away that night. She was coming with me to Nashville. She said she had gotten money from her mother's safe."

Lily's heart lurched. "The money Mrs. Keeper said my mother had stolen."

Both the Keepers turned to stare at her. "Lily?"

The sheriff handed Peterson over to one of his deputies. "Clay Lambert, I'm taking you in for questioning in the death of Noelle Keeper."

Mrs. Lambert stepped toward the sheriff. "No, you're not." She glanced around as a crowd of people started to form. Some of them held up their cell phones and took videos and photos.

"Put your cameras away," she insisted. "My son didn't kill Noelle. He's not guilty of any crime."

"Mom, it's okay." Clay tried to calm his mother. "The sheriff will find out I did nothing wrong. I loved Noelle. I never would have hurt her. And…" His voice broke. "I… I wouldn't do anything to hurt our baby."

His mother stamped her foot. "She was pregnant with Kevin's baby."

"No, Mom. The baby was mine. Noelle was carrying my child. We planned to get married."

Mrs. Lambert's face blanched. Her eyes widened. She looked around as if confused, from one person to another. "I did it for my son so he could have the career he always wanted. I scrimped and scraped to give him everything he needed, and then when his big break came, I couldn't let a spoiled rich girl take everything away from him."

Mrs. Keeper gasped. "What are you saying, Alice?"

"I'm saying I made sure Noelle wouldn't interfere with Clay becoming a star."

Lily's heart broke.

"Mom, no!" Clay reached for his mother.

"I killed her, Clay," she cried in her son's arms. "I did it for you, but I... I didn't know she was carrying your baby."

The sheriff hesitated for a long moment and then put his hand on her shoulder. "Let's go to my office, Mrs. Lambert. We can talk there. You'll need a lawyer."

He glanced back at Mrs. Keeper. "You'll need to come to my office, too. The deputy will escort you there."

Matthias wrapped his arm around Lily. "We'll close the booth and go home, Lily. We can come back for our things at a later time."

She nodded, but she kept thinking of the families who were torn apart and everything that had happened. The people who seemed so perfect had been hiding a side that she hadn't expected. She had been so hard on her mother, when her mother had been the better woman.

Her mother had wanted to give Noelle a ride that night, but Lily hadn't wanted her to stop and had argued with her mother. She was embarrassed because Mrs. Keeper had fired her mother, thinking she had stolen the money that evidently Noelle had taken. Thankfully, her mother hadn't listened to Lily and stopped anyway, but Noelle rejected the ride and said she was meeting someone. Even when her mother insisted, Noelle refused. Someone had driven by and saw them talking so rumors had spread that Lily's mother was the last person to see Noelle alive.

"I made a terrible mistake when I was a teen, Matthias. I need to go back to Pinewood and ask my mother's forgiveness. She may not realize what I'm saying, but still, I need to tell her."

"You're leaving?" he asked.

She nodded. "I have to go home."

"But—"

"And you have to let me go."

Matthias's life had turned upside down. Peterson, or Philipson, whatever his name was, had been apprehended and jailed without bail. Noelle Keeper's murder had been solved. Mrs. Lambert would stand trial for her death, and Mrs. Keeper was scheduled for a psychiatric evaluation while she was incarcerated.

Although relieved that his children would be safe walking back and forth to school, Matthias was concerned about Lily. She had been silent on the way home as if the unraveling of the murder case had been too much for her to endure.

Arriving home, she had hugged the children and then hurried into the guest room without comment.

His mother was worried and so was he. Very

worried. Lily planned to leave Sunview, and she refused to listen to his insistence that she stay.

He had given up trying to sway her. She was convinced that she needed to leave, and the idea of her leaving broke his heart. Even his mother seemed confused, yet she would be the first to remind him that Amish and *Englisch* didn't and couldn't mix. Tonight, he wondered if she was rethinking that precept of the Amish way.

He tucked the twins into bed and tried to answer their questions about Miss Lily and whether they would see her in the morning.

What could he tell them? He had no idea what her plans were or when she would leave. He wanted her to say goodbye to the children, yet he feared that parting would be too hard for them. In just the few days she had been with them, Sarah and Toby had opened their hearts to Lily. Now their hearts would be broken, just as his would be.

Matthias slept little that night. He went to the kitchen and stared through the window into the darkness. When Lily had first arrived, he had stayed awake to ensure Peterson wasn't in the area. Now he was awake because Peterson had been jailed and all had come to a good conclusion, all except Lily leaving.

Sometime between four and five in the morning, he had drifted into a fitful sleep and when he awoke some hours later, she was gone.

He woke the children for school with the news that she had left. "Will she come back?" both children had asked.

What could he tell them? He didn't know, and he didn't understand how she could have gone without saying goodbye. Yet that goodbye would have been so hard to bear. Maybe it was better this way.

"How are you, Matthias?" his mother had asked.

"Fine, *Mamm*. I'm just fine." They both knew he was trying to make light of a very difficult time.

He left the house after the children had walked to school, and he worked until sundown in the pastures, fixing broken fences and mending the troughs and areas of the barn that needed repair. He hadn't eaten, and he'd barely had anything to drink, but he didn't care. He needed to keep his body occupied and worn out so he didn't have to face the reality of a house without Lily. Duke hovered close by, but even his faithful dog couldn't heal his broken heart.

At dinner, everyone was silent and faces were downcast. His mother seemed sad as well. That night, he sat on the side of his bed and lowered his head into his hands.

"Dear, *Gott*," he said aloud, "if this woman is the one to help raise my children and if You approve of her coming into our house and becoming part of my life, then help her to decide to return. If this is not *gut* for my children, then it will not be, and I must accept the future as it comes. Know that I will always love Rachel, but love can embrace many forms, and my feelings for Lily in no way detract from my love for her. Guide me, Lord, through this difficult time so that I make wise decisions for my children, and yes, even for myself."

TWENTY-ONE

Lily stood in the driveway of her aunt's small bungalow and shoved the wad of twenty-dollar bills into Wilma's hand. "This should cover Mama's meds, then do me a favor with the extra, and buy her something nice for Christmas."

Her sweet aunt's shoulders drooped. "You hardly make enough to survive, Sugar, let alone to give me your hard-earned cash."

Lily appreciated her aunt's concern for her well-being, but she knew Wilma's social security was stretched thin and caring for Lily's mother put a strain on her aunt's already meager income.

She closed Wilma's hand around the roll of bills. "The festival at Christmas Lodge brought in extra money, and although I won't continue with my taxi business, I'll find other ways to earn my keep."

"Taxiing strangers wasn't the job I wanted for my niece, especially when you worked late into the night." Her aunt's round face tightened. "I worried about you, Sugar, and your mother would have, too, if she had realized what you were doing. There's a bad element that roams the darkness."

Lily hadn't shared everything about Peterson, although she had talked about Matthias and his family.

"If you had worked at one of the local stores or restaurants," her aunt continued, "I would have worried less."

"Being my own boss suited me just fine, Wilma."

Her aunt sighed with resignation. "You always were independent, although I guess you had to be living with your mom. Why don't you stay until Christmas?"

"It's time for me to go."

"That guy you told me about in Sunview—" Wilma leaned closer "—I know he's important to you by the look in your eyes."

Lily shrugged. "I'm not sure what's going to happen, but I'll keep you posted."

Wilma hugged her. "I'm glad you and your mother reconciled."

"God healed my heart. Evidently, He listened to your prayers."

"He listened to your prayers, as well, once you finally took time to call out to Him."

Lily smiled at the truthfulness of her aunt's statement.

"You're sure about going back?"

Lily nodded. "If they'll have me."

"And you're convinced this is what you should do?"

"I have to try to make it work. Pray for me, Auntie."

"Oh, my dear Lily, you are always in my prayers. Don't worry about your mother. She is confused at times and remembers little, but she has an inner joy that comes from letting go of worldly problems. Life was hard on Violet, but now she focuses only on the good things and the joys. She talks often of you when you were a baby and how much she loves her sweet Lily."

"I told you that I asked her forgiveness. I'm not sure if she realized what I was saying, but she smiled so proudly and then she wrapped her arms around me and hugged me tight. I cried, and she asked if she had hurt me. I told her I was the one who had hurt her, but she said her Lily Bud could never cause her pain. All Lily Bud could do was bring her abundant joy."

"You have to believe that was a moment of clarity."

"I hope it was."

"Believe it, Lily, and hold on to that moment and that beautiful, heartfelt hug."

"You'll come to see me and bring Mother."

Her aunt nodded. "Of course, as soon as you're settled and are ready for visitors. Your mother always loved the outdoors. She'll enjoy the animals and the open spaces."

Lily thought for a moment of the times they had driven past farmland when they'd moved to Macon after leaving Sunview. "She always did love farms and open spaces."

Her aunt squeezed her hand. "She would be happy knowing you're in love with an Amish man who has cattle and horses and children."

"Adorable children." The thought of Sarah and Toby warmed her heart. "Plus, Matthias does beautiful woodworking."

"He is a talented man." Again, her aunt squeezed her hand. "And a fortunate man to have you at his side."

"He may not want me."

She laughed. "I doubt that anyone could turn you down, Lily. You're a jewel."

"A precious blossom, my mother used to call me before we started to disagree about her life and my desire for independence."

"Remember the good times and forget anything that brings you pain."

"I'll take your advice."

Lily opened her car door and glanced at the back seat where she had packed a few belongings and a basket of baked goods. The world drained her, and she longed for the peace and contentment she had found in Matthias's home following the Amish way. If Matthias didn't want her, she would find a room to rent.

She kissed her aunt's cheek and waved goodbye to her mother standing in the window before she climbed into her car. After buckling her seat belt, she looked back and waved again. Her mother raised her hand, and a smile transformed her pensive gaze into the beautiful woman she had been in her youth. She waved and waved again as Lily put her car into gear and pulled onto the main road, heading up the mountain.

Leaving her mother and aunt wasn't as hard as she had expected, knowing she would see them soon. She turned her focus to the road ahead and the promise of what she might find when she arrived in Sunview.

She knew what she wanted for her life. She hoped Matthias wanted the same thing as well.

"Why did Lily leave without saying goodbye?" Sarah asked for the fourth time.

Matthias hugged her to him and patted her shoulder. "She wasn't leaving you, Sarah—" he looked at his son "—or Toby. She was leaving Sunview and some of the memories of when she was a girl. Her mother lives in Pinewood, and she went home to be with her."

"But I didn't want her to leave. I thought she liked it here. I thought she liked us."

"She liked being with you and Toby." He chucked their chins. "I feel certain of that."

He hugged both his children and then handed them their songbooks. "*Mammi* is waiting in the buggy for you. Have a *gut* time at the nursing home in town. The older people will enjoy your singing."

"*Mammi* said the nursing home is making hot chocolate for us."

Toby nodded. "And we get to decorate Christmas cookies after we sing. Then we'll give them to the residents."

"The true meaning of Christmas is in giving, which is what you're doing by giving your time and the gift of your singing to the seniors." He opened the kitchen door. "Have fun."

The children climbed in the buggy and waved goodbye as Fannie guided the mare along the drive to the main road.

Matthias returned to the kitchen. He had paperwork to complete for his woodworking business that had blossomed these last few days since the festival. Prepared to work for the next couple hours, he poured another cup of coffee, then glanced around the empty kitchen, feeling melancholy. Just days ago, Lily had been with them with her twinkling eyes and infectious laughter. The children had giggled and played games and basked in the love and attention she had showered upon them. Naturally, they were sad she had gone. Matthias was as well.

He settled into a chair at the table and studied his ledgers, but his mind kept going back to Lily. He had grieved losing Rachel; now he was grieving the loss, although completely different, of Lily. He raked his hand through his hair and wondered how long it would be until he could start to focus on work again without having Lily come to mind.

He added a list of numbers, then dropped the pencil on the table with frustration. He needed manual labor to get his thoughts in line with how life would be from now on—a life without Lily.

The sound of a car pulling into the drive confused him. Thinking it was the mailman delivering Christmas cards from distant friends and relatives, he went to the door and pulled it open.

His heart stopped. Lily slipped from her car and climbed the porch steps with a basket in hand.

"I… I didn't expect to see you again," he said.

"Merry Christmas, Matthias."

His voice hitched. "And the same to you."

She held up the basket, covered with a red-and-white gingham cloth. "I wasn't sure about Amish tradition."

He didn't understand her comment. "You mean about Christmas?"

"No." She looked down, seemingly embarrassed for some reason, and then gazed up at him, her eyes pools of wonder. "Your mother said the widow Herschberger frequently stops by with pies and cakes."

He was even more confused that she would mention the widow. "*Yah*, she does at times."

"And I know the widow Herschberger is interested in courting."

He raised his brow. "What is this about?"

"The *Englisch* have a saying that the way to a man's heart is through his stomach."

"I have heard this, *yah*."

"So the widow is trying to capture your heart with her cakes and pies."

His lips twitched, although he didn't want to jump to the wrong conclusion.

"And since the widow hopes you'll ask to court her, I thought I would express my interest as well."

"Express your interest in the widow Herschberger courting me?" He poked his thumb at his chest.

Lily's cheeks pinked. "You're making this more difficult than I expected, Matthias."

"Then please accept my apology."

She smiled, and he knew he was on the right track.

He glanced at the basket. "What have you brought me?"

She lifted the cloth. "Pecan pie, fresh cranberry and orange bread and gingerbread cookies."

"For me?"

"Yah," she slipped into the Pennsylvania Dutch response. "Although I thought the children would enjoy the cookies."

"They miss you."

"I miss them, too."

He took the basket from her hand. "Come in and we can have a slice of pie along with a cup of coffee."

"I'm not imposing?"

He shook his head. "Not at all. In fact, I was hoping to see you again."

"You wanted the baked goods?"

He put the basket on the kitchen table and then took her hand and stepped closer. "I've missed you, Lily."

"I had to see my mother."

"She's okay?"

Lily touched her forehead. "A little confused,

but in moments of clarity, we talked about the past."

"You asked her forgiveness?"

"I did, but she said there wasn't anything to forgive. I'm not sure if she was thinking clearly, but she seemed to remember what had happened that night we talked to Noelle."

Lily glanced down. "I had told my mother not to stop."

"You were hurt because she had been fired from working at the lodge."

"That's true, but I was thinking of my own pride and not about Noelle. She was pregnant and running away from her family. No matter how much she loved Clay, she must have been scared."

"It was a terrible thing that happened, but you and your mother weren't to blame. So many seemingly *gut* people made bad decisions that will impact the rest of their lives."

"I want to ensure the decisions I make from now on are well-founded."

"What kind of decisions?" He rubbed his finger along her cheek, feeling the softness of her skin.

"About the direction of my life. I... I talked to the bishop earlier today."

Not what Matthias had expected.

"I told him about my desire to become Amish."

"This is not something that often happens."

"I know. He said the same thing, but he understands my desire to embrace the faith. It will take time, and I have a lot to learn, but—"

"You have to give up your cell phone and car and all the comforts you had in Pinewood."

"But there's so much more that I will gain, Matthias."

"Oh?"

She nodded. "Especially if you decide to court me."

His heart soared. "Oh, Lily, that would make me very happy."

She stepped closer and placed her hands on his chest.

He looked into her pretty blue eyes. "I have something to tell you, Lily. Maybe it's too soon, but I can no longer keep it locked inside."

Her brow raised.

"I never thought love would come again, but you have stolen my heart." He pulled her closer. "I love you, Lily, and I want you to be my wife."

Her upturned lips broke into a beautiful smile, tears filled her eyes, but he knew they were tears of joy because his heart was overflowing with joy as well.

"Matthias, nothing would make me happier than to be your wife."

"And the children?"

"I loved them the first time I saw them."

She stretched on tiptoe and wrapped her hands around his neck as he eased his lips down to hers. His heart nearly burst as he pulled her closer and continued to kiss her, the woman he loved who one day in the not too distant future would become his wife.

"*Hallicher Grischtdaag*, Lily," he whispered. "Merry Christmas to the woman I love."

EPILOGUE

One Year Later

The twins flew down the stairs and waited on the porch as the buggy pulled into the drive. Duke barked a greeting, Sarah and Toby waved, and Fannie came outside. The smiles on their sweet faces filled Lily with joy.

She glanced at Matthias. He wrapped his arm around her waist and smiled at the tiny bundle she held in her arms. "Is the baby ready to meet her brother and sister?"

"And her *grossmuder*," Lily added. She eased back the blanket and smiled at their precious little girl. "Rosie, we're home."

The baby cooed as Matthias pulled the mare to a stop by the porch. The twins ran to the buggy. "Can we hold her?" they both asked in unison.

"Yah," Lily answered, "Once we get inside."

Fannie neared the buggy. "Let *Mammi* take

the baby." Lily carefully lowered Rosie into Fannie's outstretched arms.

"Come, children," Fannie called to Sarah and Toby. "We'll show Rosie the cradle your *datt* made for her."

The children hurried after Fannie with wide smiles and laughter. Duke followed after them.

Matthias pulled Lily close. "You've made me the happiest man in the world. This first year of our marriage has been *wunderbar*, and I know the years ahead will be as well."

"Delivering Rosie at the hospital was your idea, Matthias, but the doctor said everything went well, and for future babies, we could use a midwife." She kissed his cheek. "You don't have to worry."

"I never want anything to happen to you."

"You've given me nothing but love, Matthias. You've provided a home and a family to call my own. You love me for who I am without expecting anything in return, and you've made me so happy."

She squeezed his hand. "We met last year before Christmas and so much has happened— I became Amish, we married, then the baby born just days before our second Christmas together."

"*Gott* is so *gut*," Matthias said.

Lily agreed. "He brought me to Sunview to

find you and the children, and you've made all my dreams come true."

Matthias smiled, and her heart nearly shattered with joy as he kissed her before he helped her down from the buggy. Together, walking hand in hand, they climbed the porch steps and entered the kitchen to the sounds of Sarah's and Toby's sweet voices singing the strains of Clay Lambert's song "Home in Time for Christmas" to their new baby sister.

This Christmas, their home would be filled with three beautiful children. Lily's mother and aunt would join them for a festive meal. Gathered around the table as a family, they would give thanks for the food, then Matthias would read the story of the Christ Child's birth so long ago. Like the stable of old, their home—and their hearts—this year and in the Christmases to come would overflow with happiness and, most important of all, with love.

* * * * *

*If you've enjoyed this story,
look for these other books by Debby Giusti:*

Smugglers in Amish Country
Hidden Amish Secrets
Amish Christmas Search

Dear Reader,

When Lily Hudson returns to the hometown that banished her five years earlier, she finds herself *In a Sniper's Crosshairs*. Handsome Amish widow Matthias Overholt saves Lily once, but as he and his twin children open their hearts and their home to the pretty *Englischer*, he fears he may not be able to save her again.

I pray for my readers each day and would love to hear from you. Email me at debby@debbygiusti.com, write me c/o Love Inspired, 195 Broadway, 24th Floor, New York, NY, 10007 or visit me at www.DebbyGiusti.com and at www.facebook.com/debby.giusti.9.

As always, I thank God for bringing us together through this story.

Wishing you abundant blessings,
Debby

Get 4 FREE REWARDS!

We'll send you 2 FREE Books plus 2 FREE Mystery Gifts.

FREE
Value Over
$20

Both the **Love Inspired®** and **Love Inspired® Suspense** series feature compelling novels filled with inspirational romance, faith, forgiveness, and hope.

YES! Please send me 2 FREE novels from the Love Inspired or Love Inspired Suspense series and my 2 FREE gifts (gifts are worth about $10 retail). After receiving them, if I don't wish to receive any more books, I can return the shipping statement marked "cancel." If I don't cancel, I will receive 6 brand-new Love Inspired Larger-Print books or Love Inspired Suspense Larger-Print books every month and be billed just $6.24 each in the U.S. or $6.49 each in Canada. That is a savings of at least 17% off the cover price. It's quite a bargain! Shipping and handling is just 50¢ per book in the U.S. and $1.25 per book in Canada.* I understand that accepting the 2 free books and gifts places me under no obligation to buy anything. I can always return a shipment and cancel at any time by calling the number below. The free books and gifts are mine to keep no matter what I decide.

Choose one: ☐ **Love Inspired**
Larger-Print
(122/322 IDN GRDF)

☐ **Love Inspired Suspense**
Larger-Print
(107/307 IDN GRDF)

Name (please print)

Address   Apt. #

City   State/Province   Zip/Postal Code

Email: Please check this box ☐ if you would like to receive newsletters and promotional emails from Harlequin Enterprises ULC and its affiliates. You can unsubscribe anytime.

Mail to the **Harlequin Reader Service:**
IN U.S.A.: P.O. Box 1341, Buffalo, NY 14240-8531
IN CANADA: P.O. Box 603, Fort Erie, Ontario L2A 5X3

Want to try 2 free books from another series? Call 1-800-873-8635 or visit www.ReaderService.com.

*Terms and prices subject to change without notice. Prices do not include sales taxes, which will be charged (if applicable) based on your state or country of residence. Canadian residents will be charged applicable taxes. Offer not valid in Quebec. This offer is limited to one order per household. Books received may not be as shown. Not valid for current subscribers to the Love Inspired or Love Inspired Suspense series. All orders subject to approval. Credit or debit balances in a customer's account(s) may be offset by any other outstanding balance owed by or to the customer. Please allow 4 to 6 weeks for delivery. Offer available while quantities last.

Your Privacy—Your information is being collected by Harlequin Enterprises ULC, operating as Harlequin Reader Service. For a complete summary of the information we collect, how we use this information and to whom it is disclosed, please visit our privacy notice located at corporate.harlequin.com/privacy-notice. From time to time we may also exchange your personal information with reputable third parties. If you wish to opt out of this sharing of your personal information, please visit readerservice.com/consumerschoice or call 1-800-873-8635. **Notice to California Residents**—Under California law, you have specific rights to control and access your data. For more information on these rights and how to exercise them, visit corporate.harlequin.com/california-privacy.

LIRLIS22R2

Get 4 FREE REWARDS!

We'll send you 2 FREE Books plus 2 FREE Mystery Gifts.

FREE Value Over **$20**

Both the **Harlequin® Special Edition** and **Harlequin® Heartwarming™** series feature compelling novels filled with stories of love and strength where the bonds of friendship, family and community unite.

YES! Please send me 2 FREE novels from the Harlequin Special Edition or Harlequin Heartwarming series and my 2 FREE gifts (gifts are worth about $10 retail). After receiving them, if I don't wish to receive any more books, I can return the shipping statement marked "cancel." If I don't cancel, I will receive 6 brand-new Harlequin Special Edition books every month and be billed just $5.24 each in the U.S. or $5.99 each in Canada, a savings of at least 13% off the cover price or 4 brand-new Harlequin Heartwarming Larger-Print books every month and be billed just $5.99 each in the U.S. or $6.49 each in Canada, a savings of at least 20% off the cover price. It's quite a bargain! Shipping and handling is just 50¢ per book in the U.S. and $1.25 per book in Canada.* I understand that accepting the 2 free books and gifts places me under no obligation to buy anything. I can always return a shipment and cancel at any time by calling the number below. The free books and gifts are mine to keep no matter what I decide.

Choose one: ☐ **Harlequin Special Edition**   ☐ **Harlequin Heartwarming**
(235/335 HDN GRCQ)   **Larger-Print**
(161/361 HDN GRC3)

Name (please print)

Address   Apt. #

City   State/Province   Zip/Postal Code

Email: Please check this box ☐ if you would like to receive newsletters and promotional emails from Harlequin Enterprises ULC and its affiliates. You can unsubscribe anytime.

Mail to the **Harlequin Reader Service:**
IN U.S.A.: P.O. Box 1341, Buffalo, NY 14240-8531
IN CANADA: P.O. Box 603, Fort Erie, Ontario L2A 5X3

Want to try 2 free books from another series? Call 1-800-873-8635 or visit www.ReaderService.com.

*Terms and prices subject to change without notice. Prices do not include sales taxes, which will be charged (if applicable) based on your state or country of residence. Canadian residents will be charged applicable taxes. Offer not valid in Quebec. This offer is limited to one order per household. Books received may not be as shown. Not valid for current subscribers to the Harlequin Special Edition or Harlequin Heartwarming series. All orders subject to approval. Credit or debit balances in a customer's account(s) may be offset by any other outstanding balance owed by or to the customer. Please allow 4 to 6 weeks for delivery. Offer available while quantities last.

Your Privacy—Your information is being collected by Harlequin Enterprises ULC, operating as Harlequin Reader Service. For a complete summary of the information we collect, how we use this information and to whom it is disclosed, please visit our privacy notice located at corporate.harlequin.com/privacy-notice. From time to time we may also exchange your personal information with reputable third parties. If you wish to opt out of this sharing of your personal information, please visit readerservice.com/consumerchoice or call 1-800-873-8635. **Notice to California Residents**—Under California law, you have specific rights to control and access your data. For more information on these rights and how to exercise them, visit corporate.harlequin.com/california-privacy.

HSEHW22R2

COUNTRY LEGACY COLLECTION

EMMETT
Diana Palmer

COURTED BY THE COWBOY

THE RANCHER AND THE BABY
Marie Ferrarella

Cowboys, adventure and romance await you in this new collection! Enjoy superb reading all year long with books by bestselling authors like Diana Palmer, Sasha Summers and Marie Ferrarella!